JAMESTOWN'S AMERICAN PORTRAITS

W9-DAG-757

# All for Texas

## A Story of Texas Liberation

### G. Clifton Wisler

JAMESTOWN PUBLISHERS

a division of NTC/Contemporary Publishing Group
Lincolnwood, Illinois USA

For Gedyce McAfee, Irene Heartsill, Velma Thames, Ruby Clark, and especially Joan Jackson, who taught the love of learning.

Cover Credits
  Design: Herman Adler Design Group
  Illustration: David Schweitzer
  Timeline: (left) Library of Congress;
  (right) North Wind

ISBN: 0-8092-0588-2 (hardbound)
ISBN: 0-8092-0629-3 (softbound)

Published by Jamestown Publishers,
a division of NTC/Contemporary Publishing Group, Inc.,
4255 West Touhy Avenue,
Lincolnwood (Chicago), Illinois 60712-1975 U.S.A.
© 2000 by G. Clifton Wisler
All rights reserved. No part of this book may be reproduced,
stored in a retrieval system, or transmitted in any form or by any means,
electronic, mechanical, photocopying, recording, or otherwise,
without prior permission of the publisher.
Manufactured in the United States of America.

0 ML 0 9 8 7 6 5 4 3 2

# BYRD FAMILY TREE

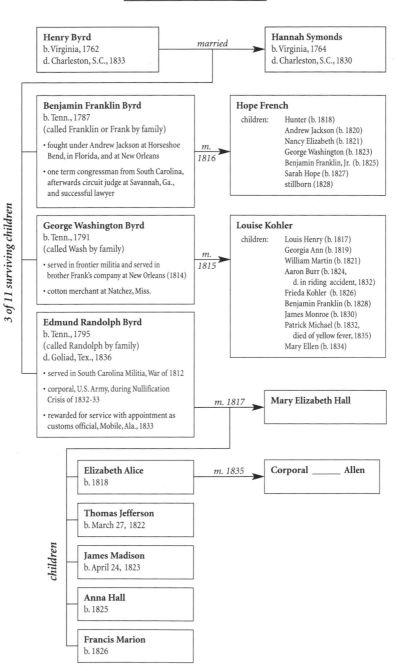

**Henry Byrd**
b. Virginia, 1762
d. Charleston, S.C., 1833

*married*

**Hannah Symonds**
b. Virginia, 1764
d. Charleston, S.C., 1830

*3 of 11 surviving children*

**Benjamin Franklin Byrd**
b. Tenn., 1787
(called Franklin or Frank by family)

• fought under Andrew Jackson at Horseshoe Bend, in Florida, and at New Orleans

• one term congressman from South Carolina, afterwards circuit judge at Savannah, Ga., and successful lawyer

*m. 1816*

**Hope French**
children:  Hunter (b. 1818)
Andrew Jackson (b. 1820)
Nancy Elizabeth (b. 1821)
George Washington (b. 1823)
Benjamin Franklin, Jr. (b. 1825)
Sarah Hope (b. 1827)
stillborn (1828)

**George Washington Byrd**
b. Tenn., 1791
(called Wash by family)

• served in frontier militia and served in brother Frank's company at New Orleans (1814)

• cotton merchant at Natchez, Miss.

*m. 1815*

**Louise Kohler**
children:  Louis Henry (b. 1817)
Georgia Ann (b. 1819)
William Martin (b. 1821)
Aaron Burr (b. 1824, d. in riding accident, 1832)
Frieda Kohler (b. 1826)
Benjamin Franklin (b. 1828)
James Monroe (b. 1830)
Patrick Michael (b. 1832, died of yellow fever, 1835)
Mary Ellen (b. 1834)

**Edmund Randolph Byrd**
b. Tenn., 1795
(called Randolph by family)
d. Goliad, Tex., 1836

• served in South Carolina Militia, War of 1812

• corporal, U.S. Army, during Nullification Crisis of 1832-33

• rewarded for service with appointment as customs official, Mobile, Ala., 1833

*m. 1817*

**Mary Elizabeth Hall**

*children*

**Elizabeth Alice**
b. 1818

*m. 1835*

**Corporal _____ Allen**

**Thomas Jefferson**
b. March 27, 1822

**James Madison**
b. April 24, 1823

**Anna Hall**
b. 1825

**Francis Marion**
b. 1826

# Texas 1836

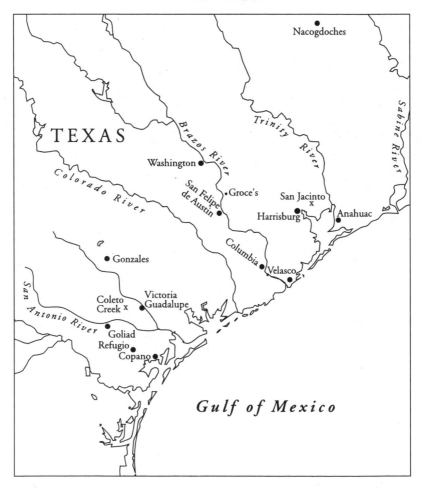

# Chapter 1

## Itchy Feet

I suppose you could say that the urge to move started with Grandpa Henry. He was, as Pa liked to say, the first of the Byrds to take flight. Not that they were much for running away. Henry Byrd fought the British at Cowpens, and he had kin fighting redcoats and Indians from Chesapeake Bay to the Ohio Valley. Two of Pa's brothers were with Andy Jackson himself when he thrashed the British Army outside of New Orleans. Pa, being the youngest, missed that fight, but he served in both the militia and the regular army later on. So you see, we Byrds may tend to have itchy feet as far as settling down is concerned, but we're not shy on backbone.

Once, a few years back, when we were living in Charleston, South Carolina, three boys chased me five city blocks toward the docks. Each one of them was a head taller and three years older than I was, and I confess to being a little scared. The tallest one, Rufe Keller, had a stone big as my head in his hand, and he was plum determined to crack my skull with it. Now, I wasn't 10 years old at the time, but even then I wouldn't be chased for very long. I turned a corner, stopped, and picked up a cobblestone out of the street. When those three boys made the turn, I hurled my rock right past old Rufe's ear.

Well, Ma said that wasn't the smartest thing a boy had ever done, but it did get their attention. "I'm not afraid of you!" I hollered as I picked up a second rock. My aim was better this time, and I clipped Alfred Murdock's right elbow. He gave a yelp and beat a hasty retreat, dragging his brother Sam along. I'd like to say I set Rufe to running too, but the truth is that he pounced on me and pounded me proper. He didn't stop until my right eye was growing purple and blood dribbled out of the corner of my mouth.

"Who's right now?" Rufe shouted.

"I don't know for sure, but you *aren't*," I answered.

The funniest thing happened then. He rolled away, stood up, and helped me to my feet. I was bumped and bleeding, but he hadn't won anything. We both knew it too.

"Well," Rufe told me, "a fellow who'll take a whipping for what he believes ought not to lose more than a little blood."

Afterward, nobody bothered me much. My sister Beth told me it was because Rufe let it be known he would thrash anybody who did. I didn't understand why until much later, after the fray at Goliad. I'm getting ahead of myself, though.

I passed the first 10 years of my life in Charleston, and they were mostly happy years. Pa was a corporal in the United States Army, stationed at Fort Moultrie. That's the fort where the Colonials had given the British a drubbing during the Revolution. He met Ma right after joining the regulars, back in 1817. She was a sergeant's daughter, and she told us a few tales of how they had to sneak past her father's post to pass time together. Beth was born a year after they were married. Then on March 27, 1822, I— Thomas Jefferson Byrd—saw the light of day.

Ma said I came out squawking and have been doing so ever since. Well, I don't know that I'd agree to that. But I do know that it took all the will a boy could muster to survive Beth's torments those first few years. I can't really blame her, though. She had had the run of the little wooden house that Pa rented until the rest of us started arriving. James Madison was next, a year and a month after me. Anna Hall, named after Ma's grandmother, came two years after that. A year later Francis Marion Byrd, whom we call Frank, finished out the family. He was named for the Swamp Fox.

If I came out squawking, I don't know what you would say about my brother Frank's arrival. There was hollering and shouting and plenty of running around. Ma was in bed for close to a month afterward. She called his birth a rough hatching, and the whole family was worried about her and little Frank both. That was the time when

Grandpa Henry and Grandma Hannah came to help look after us.

"Sure, it's mighty crowded, but it's crowded in a good way," Beth remarked.

I was just four at the time and wouldn't have known one way or the other. Ma's hard time mellowed Beth considerably, though, and afterward she treated us more like an old mother hen watching over some scrawny chicks.

Like I said, Charleston was a pretty good place. There was always something going on. If it wasn't a carnival, it was a fair. If life at our little house got too peaceful, you could wander down to the waterfront and watch the ships sailing in or out of the harbor. Grandpa Henry took us down to the wharf and taught us all how to fish. Grandma Hannah took on our education. She died just before Christmas 1830, and Grandpa followed her the day after I turned 11. I had never felt crowded in our little house, even with two brothers sharing a bed that I could have filled on my own. The place felt different after Grandma Hannah died, and it was downright empty when Grandpa Henry left us.

"It's time we moved on," Pa announced that May of 1834. "I've seen enough of army life to know I'm ready for something different."

Twenty years was a long time to stay at anything, to my way of thinking, so I wasn't all that surprised. The truth was that Pa had sort of worn out his welcome in Charleston. Andy Jackson, who had been elected president of the whole country then, had used the army to enforce a new tariff law. South Carolina had almost gone to war over it. The hotheads said that any state that didn't like one of General Andy's laws didn't have to obey it, and South Carolina came close to pulling itself right out of the country. After a lot of talk and a little shooting by the grown-ups, not to mention a few fights by us youngsters, the whole thing was sorted out. The President collected his customs duties, Pa got his sergeant's stripes, and South Carolina kept its star on the flag.

People, even some of the soldiers, looked on Pa as a turncoat of sorts, though. While the soldiers who were born up North were mostly ignored, Pa and a handful of Southern-born regulars were treated with taunts, insults, and worse. The final straw came when old Mrs. Hawkins, our landlady, turned us out of the house we'd been renting since Beth was born.

"Like I said," Pa declared when he got the news, "time to move on."

So Pa resigned from the army and took a new job with the customs office down in Mobile, Alabama. I figured the president owed him a favor. We sailed around the tip of Florida and arrived there three weeks before Christmas 1834. Pa's new job gave him enough money to buy us our own house, and he even managed to send Madison and me to a proper school.

Now I ought to explain about the name business right here. Grandpa Henry liked to name his children after famous folk, but he had the odd habit of calling them by their middle names. Pa had two brothers, Benjamin Franklin Byrd and George Washington Byrd, but I'd never in all my life heard either man called by his first name. It was always Uncle Frank or Uncle Wash. It was no different with my brother Madison and me. Using my first name, Tom, would have saved considerable time when I was scribbling my name on school papers, but the best I could arrange was for my siblings to call me T. J. Ma wouldn't abide anybody calling himself by initials, though. She also wouldn't have a son of hers called Marion, either. When I said that Francis wasn't much better than Marion, little Frank escaped the family curse and got to have a normal name. As for the girls, Beth did what she liked, and little Annie benefited from Frank's breakthrough.

Mobile was a strange sort of place compared to Charleston. The southern part of Alabama had been a part of Spanish Florida, and a lot of Spanish traditions hung on. Some of the people spoke Spanish or French better than English, and Pa picked up a smattering of each language working at the customs office. It was in Mobile that I learned about Mardi Gras, which is French for "Fat Tuesday." It was the big celebration that Catholics had before the Lenten season started. Lent had to do with the way Catholics sacrificed before they celebrated Easter, and I never did figure it all out. Mobile celebrated the day in high fashion, though, with parties and masked parades. Mardi Gras was almost as good as Christmas was—a sort of holiday from school, full of fun and games.

I would like to have seen more than one Mardi Gras

celebration, but it wasn't to be. Mobile, being on the Gulf of Mexico, was subject to strong storms and seasonal fevers. In the short time that we lived there (just over a year), somebody was always sick. Also during that summer of 1835, yellow fever swept through the Mississippi delta country and plagued the coast. My little cousin Patrick—who lived up in Natchez, Mississippi— died of it. Ma was never comfortable in Mobile after that, and Pa was talking about moving on too. His work was tiresome, and there was a lot of talk about free land to be had in the American settlements in Texas.

Texas was a place that excited the imagination. Even Aaron Burr, who had been a vice-president of the United States, had thought to carve himself an empire out of the place. Texas had long been part of Spain, but then so had Florida, Mobile, and even New Orleans for a time. The eastern part of Texas was mostly wild forest and prairie before a Missourian named Moses Austin had the notion to settle Americans there. His son Stephen put the plan into action, though. And, following its own Revolution back in 1821, the new nation of Mexico allowed the Americans to settle there.

Pa first spoke of Texas that July of 1835, but Ma wasn't interested in leaving a little gulf port like Mobile for a wilderness full of hungry bears and savage Indians. She had cousins living in Montgomery, the Alabama capital, and that was where she wanted to move.

"And what would I do to support us?" Pa asked. "Be a clerk in your cousin's law office? Mary, it's lawyers that make my job here so hard!"

I knew what Pa meant. Half of my classmates at Mr.
Peterson's little school were lawyers' sons. Mr. Peterson
himself once said that half the lawyers in creation had
come to Alabama. In the fall of 1835, one of those
lawyers, also a South Carolinian by birth, came to Mobile.
He changed my world forever.

James Butler Bonham wasn't even 30 years old when
he appeared in Mobile with a letter asking for volunteers
to go to Texas to protect the American settlers from the
cruel threats posed by Mexico's new dictator, Antonio
López de Santa Anna. Pa took me to hear Lieutenant
Bonham talk, and I confess that when he was finished I
was ready to go to Texas myself. He painted a wonderful
picture of Texas, a land of green valleys and wide rivers,
where horses and cattle wandered freely and where
Americans had planted rich crops of cotton and wheat and
corn.

His brow was knitted as he described the merciless
Santa Anna, who had seized authority, jailed Stephen
Austin, and sent a Mexican Army to take possession of
Texas. The lieutenant spoke glowingly of his old friend
Colonel Buck Travis, who was determined to defend the
settlements and was already marching on the key Mexican
army at San Antonio de Bexar. With a flourish, Lieutenant
Bonham snatched off his fine beaver hat and waved it
westward.

"Are there men here with the spirit of Washington, of
Marion, of Greene?" Bonham called. "Are there men cut
from the cloth of Andrew Jackson, willing to stand up to

the rockets and cannons of a merciless enemy? Are there men here prepared to risk all for a chance to build a new nation out of the rough and untamed West?"

Bonham added that each volunteer would be furnished with transportation and that grants of land almost beyond imagination could be won by joining the fight.

"Did you hear that, Jefferson?" Pa asked. "Land of my own! A fair and honorable fight followed by a future for my family."

Well, Ma didn't see it that way, and she was dead set against any such nonsense as Pa marching off with the band of men Lieutenant Bonham was organizing. He only had a couple dozen men in all, and that made for a mighty small army. On top of that, Ma argued that the promise of land wouldn't mean a thing if Bonham and Travis and the rest of them lost. "How many men have gone into Texas set on conquering the place and have found only a grave?" she shouted.

I didn't know what she was talking about, but Mr. Peterson did. It seemed that Aaron Burr wasn't the only would-be king of Texas. Before Mexican independence a handful of others had tried to take control of the place. Each time they tried, a Spanish army had marched out, fought them, and shot those who survived the battle.

"But there's a difference this time," he told me. "This isn't a matter of some fool trying to steal a country. What Lieutenant Bonham wants are volunteers to help protect peaceful settlers from an oppressive government."

"Are you thinking of going?" I asked him.

9

"I have a young wife and two little girls, Jefferson," he answered. "I would, but who could shoulder my responsibilities here at the school? Who would take care of my little girls if the unthinkable occurred and I were killed?"

I pondered those same questions that night as I followed Pa through the front door and out onto the veranda.

"Mr. Peterson says Ma's right," I told him. "You only get the land if you win. Twenty men aren't enough to stop an army. Andy Jackson didn't stop the British by himself, you know."

"Look up there, son," Pa said, pointing to the sky. For days the whole country had been alive with talk of a wondrous comet streaming across the evening sky. It was up there, all right, just as that English fellow Halley had predicted. Most everyone thought it was an omen of great things to come.

"You think it's a sign, Pa?" I asked.

"Your grandpa would have seen it that way." He motioned me closer, and I moved over so that he could rest his hands on my shoulders. "Sometimes a man sees an open door that offers him a chance to play a part in making history. Oh, I don't mean he'll be a great general or even a leader at all. History may seem to be made solely by generals and presidents, but it's really the individual men and women who make things happen. Did your grandpa ever tell you how he and his neighbors picked up their rifles, marched through the mountains, and defeated

the British and the Tories at King's Mountain and the
Cowpens?"

"No, sir," I answered.

"It isn't a pretty story and it's not so well known as
Yorktown or Saratoga. But in the end it's the small fights
that make the victory possible. Your grandpa and others
like him—boys really—left their homes and came out of
the hills that are now Tennessee to join Virginians and
Carolinians. Together they made up a few hundred
untrained mountaineers, but they did what two
Continental armies had been unable to do: they stopped
the British and their Tory friends cold. Most of them went
back home afterward, but the deed had been done. Lord
Cornwallis had to move north, and Washington trapped
him at Yorktown."

"How do you know so much about all that, Pa? I don't
think I've ever seen you pick up a book."

"I didn't have a school to go to when I was a boy," he
explained. "Truth be told, I can't read very well in spite of
all my ma's efforts. But I listened to my own pa when he
talked of what he'd done and what he'd seen. I listened
when the old-timers gathered around our fire to chat. And
I've seen one or two things myself."

"Are we going to Texas then?"

"I sense a door opening, son. I don't entirely trust in
signs, but I know my heart. If there are people in trouble,
people struggling for freedom, then I think I should do
what I can do to help. Maybe no one will know that
Randolph Byrd was there, but I would know if he wasn't."

"Yes, sir."

"You'll feel a considerable burden yourself, Jefferson. You will have to see your mother and brothers and sister safely to Texas—maybe do the first planting yourself. You'll be the man of the family."

I hadn't considered that, and I shuddered. Pa noticed, and he lifted my chin so that I could see the comet overhead.

"It's a wondrous thing, don't you think?" he asked.

"It's bright, all right."

"Something is bound to come of such a sight, Jefferson. And I feel the need to be a part of whatever that is."

# Chapter 2

## Texas

They called themselves the Mobile Grays, the little band of volunteers who followed Lieutenant Bonham aboard ship. I believe that if it hadn't been for that comet, Ma might have talked Pa out of going. She herself had a terrible dread of his leaving.

"I dreamed of long winter nights alone in my room," she told him. "I dreamed of so much thunder and fire."

"You had dreams before we came to Mobile," Pa told her. "I'll miss you too, but we won't be apart a long time, dear."

She felt otherwise, but Pa would not be diverted from the path he had chosen. Lieutenant Bonham had named him a sergeant, as he was the most experienced among the volunteers and the oldest by 10 years at least. Some of those going were scarcely older than I was, and half had yet to start using a razor. Nevertheless, they marched

aboard ship in high spirits, singing and waving farewell. I'd
bet half the unmarried ladies in Mobile were there to bid
them adieu.

Pa had been more right about my burden than I ever
could have imagined. I should have known something was
going on when he didn't mention Beth helping to look
after the family. Well, no sooner did we see Pa off than
Beth announced she was returning to South Carolina. For
weeks she had been keeping company with a certain
Corporal Allen. She wasn't even 18 yet, and I was struck
dumb when she told me she had decided to marry the
corporal and return with him to South Carolina.

"Beth, we need you," I argued. "There's too much for
me to do alone."

"Oh, Ma will do all the hard work, T. J. And Maddy
will prove as useful as you are with farm work. He's helped
with Ma's garden, and he knows how to harness coach
horses. You can barely stay in a saddle."

"I haven't had that many chances," I objected. "And
anyway, what do you know about this corporal?"

"Enough," she insisted. "I love him. His family has
land we can farm. Don't you see, T. J.? This is the start of
*my* adventure."

I looked at Ma for support, but she seemed well
pleased with Beth's decision.

"If the worst happens, I may need to send Anna and
Frank to you for a time," she said to Beth. "They're young.
I don't like thinking of them cold and hungry."

I could see how much use they both thought I would

be. It ate at me. But as the days passed, so did our worst fears. Pa wrote from Texas that the Mobile Grays had arrived just in time to celebrate the surrender of the Mexican army. The Texians had captured all the old Spanish forts and sent the Mexicans scrambling south. General Martin Perfecto de Cos, the dictator's own brother-in-law, had signed a parole and given up his army's weapons and ammunition. Cos agreed to lead his men south of the Rio Grande and fight no more in Texas.

We remained in Mobile long enough for Ma to arrange the sale of our house and to buy some things that we would need to plant a crop on our land in Texas. After bidding farewell to Mr. Peterson and my schoolmates, I packed my own few belongings and helped my brothers and sister do the same. Beth had already left by then, and I felt lonelier than I had at any other moment in my whole life.

"How will we manage everything by ourselves?" I asked Ma.

"You'll have your brothers and little Anna to help you," she replied. "Jefferson, it's only when you're on you own—when there's no one there to do for you—that you discover how strong you truly are. None of us would do very well by ourselves, but together we will survive until your father joins us."

We sailed to New Orleans and then on to Texas. We arrived at Velasco at the mouth of the Brazos River in mid-January 1836. The weather was unseasonably cold, and we felt no warmer when we were greeted by the Texians. No one there seemed to have authority to grant us any land, we hadn't a friend within a hundred miles, and news of Pa and the Mobile Grays was sketchy at best.

"What do we do now?" I asked Ma.

"Hope for a miracle," she answered.

The miracle, as it happened, turned out to be a friendly Tennessee-born woman named Mamie Sagler and her spindly-legged son, Josh. Mrs. Sagler's husband and her two oldest sons, Sam and Seth, were off with the Texian army, so she had room for strays in her home upriver.

"I've got a man named Moses who is the best carpenter in Texas," she declared when we started the journey up the Brazos to her place south of Columbia. "He and Josh can help you put up a house once the weather clears. There is plenty of good land hereabouts for sale, and I expect we can sort that out. Once the fighting's over, your husband will have land granted him, and you may want to move. If so, you'll find a good price for a house close to the river. Lord knows, there will be more pilgrims like yourselves."

The trip upriver was better than 20 miles, and Ma remarked with wonderment at the ease with which Josh and his ma managed it on their own.

"Only way to get supplies is to get down to the coast," Mrs. Sagler explained. "I'd send Josh by himself, but he hasn't learned to haggle well enough. He's a kind-hearted soul, and I don't fault him for that. But it leads to bad business practices."

Josh told me later that she was talking about the time

he gave away two chickens to a hungry family in Velasco. "They looked as though they hadn't eaten anything in days," he said, "and Ma herself would have stopped, cooked up the chickens for them, and probably taken them into the house for a month. But I do it, and all she can do is complain that I'm eating into her profits."

I didn't much like the notion that *we* might be a charity case, but I confess I was relieved to find some kindness. I couldn't help liking it at the Sagler place. Josh was 15, and his twin brothers Andy and Spence—who had stayed home to mind the farm—were 11. There was no mistaking any of them for their mother's boys. All the Saglers had reddish-blond hair, and I never had seen boys with so many freckles. They had green eyes, which Grandpa Henry always told me were a sign of good fortune. To judge the Sagler place from a distance, you would believe it. There were two barns, one for dairy cows and the other for storing fodder. The house was two stories high, and it could sleep 20 people in a pinch. Ma and Anna shared the guest room. Maddy, Frank, and I were supposed to take Seth's room, but Josh argued his ma and mine into letting me bunk with him.

"That's Sam's bed there," Josh explained when he showed me the room. "He's off with the Army—Pa and Seth too. The house seems just about deserted sometimes, what with all of them gone. Then the twins wake up, and things start happening."

"You don't have to tell me about brothers," I told Josh. "Frank's little and stays out of the way most of the time, but Maddy can vex me sometimes! I swear, he knows just the right things to say to get me mad."

"Yeah, that's a brother, all right," Josh agreed.

Josh and I took an instant shine to each other. He knew so many things, and he taught me a little something every day. I think he liked that. At any rate, he started calling me Jeff, which was better than Jefferson or Birdie or some of the other things I'd been called in my life. Working alongside Josh, I was a lot more help than I could have been on my own, I think.

Beth had been right about Maddy. He took to farm chores as though he was born for them. He did know plants and horses. We weren't there a week before he proved himself twice as useful as me. He would go out early with the Sagler twins and milk the cows. He taught me how to slop the hogs a day after he had learned from watching Josh. As for horses, he managed to calm Mrs. Sagler's team and coax them into the barn the afternoon that we had our first bad Texas storm.

I'd heard it was hot in Texas, but nobody had said what winters were like there. That January on the Brazos was harder than any I'd known in the Carolinas, and the storms were as fierce as any I'd seen in Mobile. The weather was changeable too. I remember one day when the sun came out and the air got almost tolerable. Then a bank of clouds swept in, the wind came howling up, and hailstones as big as peanuts battered the roof.

"That's nothing," Josh said, laughing. "I once saw a hailstone so big we put Pa's hat atop it and figured there must be some man frozen underneath!"

I might have believed him, but redheads make bad liars. They can't keep from laughing at their own jokes.

It was the day after the hailstorm that I met Moses and his son Abner. I had wondered how Mrs. Sagler would leave two boys home alone when she went out on her errands, and I quickly found my answer. Moses, his wife Harriet, and Abner lived in their own little house a half-mile upriver from the main house. Whenever Mrs. Sagler left, they came up to watch the place.

"Moses can make anything," Josh had explained when we were on our way to meet him. "He operates a small sawmill, making oak planks and such. He makes furniture for us to sell in town."

"Is he kin?" I asked.

Josh gave me a stare like I had asked the dumbest question in tarnation.

"You're from Mobile?" he asked.

"Lately, but mostly I lived in Charleston," I explained.

"South Carolina?"

I nodded.

"Don't they have slaves there?"

It hit me like a board. A family as prosperous as the Saglers would have owned slaves in Mobile or Charleston. Somehow I never considered it, though. There had been black men unloading crates at Velasco, just as there were at Mobile and New Orleans.

"I've seen slaves," I said, "but we never owned any. Truth is, I never even spoke to one."

"Well, no matter what anybody's told you, they don't bite," Josh said, slapping me on the back. "Watch you don't track dirt on Harriet's floor, though, or you might wish they did. She swings a mean broom!"

Actually, Harriet was down at the river, doing the wash. Moses, a tall, broad-shouldered man in his late 30s, gripped my hand firmly and welcomed me to Texas. Abner, who was maybe 17, did likewise.

"Ma figures we can maybe spare wood for them to put up a house," Josh said. "We'll have some trees to clear, but I figure that little rise just south of the big house will do. Pa hasn't cleared the land along the river there, so he'd likely part with it."

"Your mama figure it that way too?" Moses asked.

"I don't plan to put up two houses, Moses," Josh replied. "You know I never volunteer for extra work."

"Yeah, we do know that," Abner said, grinning.

"Just how big a house do you want, Mr. Byrd?" Josh asked, turning to me. "You figure a regular dog run or maybe a square with rooms in each corner and a hall between?"

"I don't know," I said, confused. "Has Ma said something? I thought Moses was just going to help us this spring, once the fighting's all over and the men have come back."

"You built a lot of houses, have you?" Moses asked.

"I can't even make a proper kite," I replied. "I put together a fair rowboat once, but it sank first time out."

Moses laughed, and even Josh cracked a grin.

"I figure you and maybe Madison can help some," Josh said, leading me out the door. "Moses and Abner will do the framing. We wouldn't want that house blowing away in the first good storm."

Myself, I could have stayed all winter and most of the spring at the Sagler house without giving it a second thought. But when I brought up the subject with Ma, it was clearly decided.

"We'll be better neighbors than company," she explained. "I've already arranged the price of the lumber with Mrs. Sagler, and we'll order the window glass next week. You do what you can to help. Madison will help with the farm chores, and I'll do some sewing to pay our keep."

"Yes, ma'am," I replied.

"Jefferson, you treat those black people right too. You know your pa and I don't abide anybody mistreating slaves."

"Don't worry, Ma," Maddy said, poking his head through the doorway. "The only one he mistreats is me."

I gave him a fierce look, but he only laughed.

"You go easy on your brothers," Ma urged. "They've got some hard days ahead too. . . . Don't go too easy, though," she added with a wink.

And so it was that I learned how to build a house. Ma decided she wanted a dog-run cabin, an odd sort of house that was fashionable among Texians. You put up two squares on either side of a wooden floor and put a roof over the whole thing. The joke was that the porch was for the dogs to run through.

"Ma, I don't see the sense of it," I told her. "We don't have any dogs."

"Got plenty of boys, though," she told me. "They need room to run too."

Actually, the design made sense. If your family got bigger, you just closed up the center and had an extra room. In summer a welcome breeze swept through, and the children often slept outside.

The only real hard work was clearing the oak and cedar trees from the hillside and dragging rocks up from the river to make fireplaces. Moses and Abner built the fireplaces by using a sort of mud, straw, and cow-dung mixture between the flat stones. They also made the foundation of stones, which they covered with floorboards. Then they framed the two squares, framed the doors and windows, and blocked out the roof. Josh and I cut the shingles ourselves out of cedar logs.

Any day the weather was decent, the four of us would be out on that hill, working away at the house. Except for two days wasted while waiting on window glass, we made relatively short work of it. Ma and Annie made all the curtains themselves, while Maddy, Frank, and I painted the house an odd shade of blue.

"It was the least expensive paint we could find," Ma explained. It dried the color of an angry sky, and I couldn't help laughing. She promised we'd improve on it once Pa got his discharge from the Army of Texas.

Thinking back, we built that house and got settled

into it remarkably fast. Almost a month to the day we'd
landed at Velasco, we gathered with the Saglers and two or
three other neighbor families to mark our house's
completion.

"Odd color," Mrs. Hamilton remarked. "A little yellow
trim would help."

"You'll want a stable for the horses too," her husband
added. "A man looks after his stock with care."

I knew those words were aimed my way, and I bit my
tongue. It was only later, when Wes, one of the Hamilton
boys, laughed at Ma's curtains, that I took offense.

"We might've done better if Pa was here," I said
between clenched teeth. "We heard you Texians were in
trouble, so we came to help. Other than the Saglers, it
looks like most of you people are standing back and letting
others do your fighting."

Well, Wes was nearer Josh's age than mine, and he
wasn't inclined to let a smaller boy get away with such
words. He threw off his coat and came at me. I stood my
ground and drove an angry fist into his gut. He might
have been half a head taller than me, but he collapsed in a
heap.

"That won't win you any friends," Josh whispered.
Then he added, "Wish I'd done it myself."

Our fight was short lived. Wes had two older brothers
there who came to his aid, but Mrs. Sagler had seen and
heard it all. She shouted us quiet, waved the Hamiltons
toward their wagon, and grabbed me by the ear. Shortly I
was sitting meekly beside Ma on the porch of our odd-

blue house.

"You should understand how it is," Mrs. Hamilton told us the next morning when she brought over a pie as peace offering. "Some of us have been out here more than 10 years. We've seen these Mexican presidents come and go. They stamp and storm, but in the end we early settlers are not enough trouble for the Mexicans to bother with. It's all these people pouring in here from the States who will alarm the government. Don't you see? We're not Americans, we Hamiltons. In order to keep Columbia out of the fighting, we've sworn oaths to the government of Mexico. All these American hotheads like Buck Travis and Sam Houston are newcomers. They don't speak for Texas. And I fear that in the end we'll pay a high price for their actions. They can *go* home. We *are* home."

"Are you saying that Pa and the others came here for nothing?" I asked.

"Jefferson, I think some men have come with the best intentions, but most have come with the worst. Good, honest souls believe in constitutions and laws, but many have simply come to grab land and wealth. My husband met General Santa Anna when Santa Anna was a young man. He knows that the general's not the sort of man to take a slap in the face, and that's what the seizure of the forts will seem to him. He'll come back. And when he does, I hope there are more than a few Alabamans to stop him."

# Chapter 3

## Bound for Goliad

I wish I had paid more attention to Mrs. Hamilton. She was the only person I ever talked to who understood what was really going on that winter. Pa sure didn't. He wrote us a letter in late February about the chaos that had overtaken the army. There were no less than three men who each thought they were in command. Two different bunches had set off toward the Mexican town of Matamoros, stripping the old Spanish presidio La Bahia at Goliad of everything. Pa pleaded with us to send any food or clothing we could spare to the garrison at once.

Around Columbia there was a lot of talk about some sort of assembly at Washington, a little town upriver. Josh told me there was going to be a government put together. If anything was happening at all, it didn't seem to help the army. Nobody rushed any reinforcements westward,

either. A lot of people said there wasn't any big hurry—
that the Mexicans were busy putting down other revolts
and wouldn't spare troops to send to Texas.

The fact that nobody besides us was worried about Pa
bothered me considerably. Ma was forever writing letters
hoping to do some good, but there wasn't any regular
mail, so most of the letters sat in a pile atop the small
writing desk that Moses had crafted for her.

We received worse news before long. Lieutenant
Bonham was with Colonel Travis and Jim Bowie at an old
mission called the Alamo at San Antonio. Thousands of
Mexican soldiers had arrived, and they had everyone really
worried.

"It's not possible," Mrs. Sagler said, shaking her head.
"Nobody could have made the march from Mexico to San
Antonio in winter, even in mild weather. This has been a
killing winter."

Nevertheless, the Mexicans had done it, and more of
them were rumored to be on the way. The folks around
Columbia offered flour, salted beef, bacon, and beans for
the garrison at Goliad. The trouble was finding a
volunteer to take it to the men there.

"My pa and brothers are at Goliad," Josh announced
when he stopped at our place with a wagon. "I've got four
good horses, and I know the way. What I need is
somebody to spell me—talk to me and keep me going—so
we can cover the distance fast. Well, Jeff? Your pa's there
too, isn't he?"

"You mean leave now, today?" I asked. "I don't see
how—"

"You think you can't leave because your ma and family need you," Josh said, his eyes full of worry. "Listen, if those Mexican soldiers starve our army out of the fort, a boy or two on the Brazos won't be worth a penny. We can get these supplies to La Bahia and be a real help."

I could have argued with the words but not with Josh's eyes. I ran to the house to tell Ma. She was out back making soap, so I paused long enough in the house to kiss Annie and give little Frank a hug. Then I walked back and took Madison aside.

"Maddy, I've got to go with Josh and take food to Pa," I told him. "Nobody else is willing to do it, so we have to. Understand?"

He stared at me in surprise, then brushed a mop of brown hair out of his eyes and grabbed my arm.

"Don't," he pleaded. "I've heard people talking. They don't think any of the soldiers are coming home, T. J."

"Maddy, I've got to try," I told him. "You'll tend to things?"

"Better'n you could," he told me. I tried to lift his spirits, but he was only 11, and I'd dumped a heavier load onto him than Pa had left me. I didn't have the words in me that would make him feel any better.

"Ma?" I called.

"Can't you see I'm busy?" she said, stirring the kettle. "I thought you were going to chop kindling. I swear, Jefferson—"

She saw the dour look on my face and swallowed her words. I could tell she was expecting bad news, but she wasn't prepared for what I told her.

"No!" she shouted, abandoning her work and storming to my side. She gripped my shoulders so hard that it hurt. "I won't have it! Jefferson, there are grown boys and men to do that job. You're only 13!"

"They don't have a pa hungry for want of something we can give him," I told her. "Josh and I will make a quick trip of it. You saw how we got down to Velasco and back last week."

"And if Mexican soldiers find you on the road?"

"I haven't heard they're shooting boys yet," I answered. "If I stay home, Josh will go alone. He won't be half as likely to make it by himself. I'm not much use here. Madison's more help with chores. Besides, I figure we owe Mrs. Sagler for all her help."

If I hadn't added that last part, I don't believe Ma would have allowed it. We both knew how much we owed the woman with the big house and the even bigger heart. I didn't need much squirming room, and Ma gave it to me. I slipped away, then paused and walked back to tell her I'd bring Pa back safely. "I love you," I said, kissing her cheek. "I remember what you said about hard times building up a person. I'll just have to build myself up a little more."

"Don't grow so tall that I don't recognize you," she said. Her eyes leaked tears, and I couldn't stand seeing her so unhappy. I waved Maddy to her and ran back into the house. I only took time enough to grab a couple of blankets and my coat. Then I raced down the hill and climbed up beside Josh.

"It's going to be hard," he whispered.

"On us or on them?" I asked.

"On all of us," he told me. He was on target there.

The little town of Goliad was better than a hundred miles away. We had no map, and there was scarcely anything resembling a real road through that part of Texas. The rutted trail we followed southwestward had to be the right way.

"The Mexicans cut the first trail through here," Josh explained as he urged the horses along. "Mainly it was for soldiers to move from this place to that. There's another road to the old mission town of Nacogdoches. Besides those roads, there are mainly rivers to connect the settlements."

"And you're sure we're going the right way?"

"I've been this way twice," Josh explained. "Once I went as far as Guadalupe Victoria. We traded some lumber for cattle there. Goliad's just south of there."

"I'd feel better about that if I saw a map."

"I've got the map in my head, Jeff."

"Well, I can't read it when it's in there."

"You don't have to. Just spell me and keep the wagon on the trail."

The more I ran those words through my head, the more it seemed like pure foolishness. Two boys heading out alone with heaven only knows what ahead of them! No map! No help! But whenever I started to object, I remembered the words of Pa's letter and my promise to Ma. This time I had to be strong and get the job done. Pa was depending on me.

Actually, we did fairly well at first. As we passed one little settlement after another, people added what food they could spare. Sometimes folks would ride along for a time. They were especially helpful getting us across rivers, and we had plenty of those to cross. Winter storms had flooded the Colorado well past its banks, but a fellow who lived upstream led us to a reliable ford. I worried that water might get to the flour, but he showed us how to caulk the boards and protect the cargo. In the end, we got across just fine.

The short days made every second of daylight precious, and we barely paused unless a fallen tree blocked our way. Sometimes the road bogged down in mud, and we had to get out and push the wagon out of its own ruts. Even so, three days after leaving the Brazos, we arrived at Guadalupe Victoria, capital of the de Leon Colony.

We crossed the Guadalupe River as the sun was settling into the western horizon.

"How far does that map in your head say we are from Goliad?" I asked Josh.

"Maybe six hours with fresh horses," he answered. "And fresh drivers. We'd better make camp."

"If we went on, we'd be there a little after midnight," I argued.

"We wouldn't be any such thing," Josh replied. "The road's pretty good here near town, but that doesn't mean it's good up ahead. I don't know what's ahead, and neither do you."

"We could go a little farther. That way we could head out first thing in the morning."

"We could probably talk our way into a warm bed under a solid roof here in town."

I confess it was tempting, but I shook my head. Josh shrugged his shoulders and nudged the horses back into motion.

We traveled maybe eight miles farther before stopping. By then the night was pitch black, the road was mostly ruts, and even I had to admit we couldn't continue. Josh lit a candle, but a haze shrouded the ground and we could see almost nothing. I unhitched the horses and staked them out a short distance away. There was some grass there, but it was mostly frozen. I opened a bag of oats for the horses to chew. Josh found a shallow stream just ahead and filled some water buckets for them. We then sat in the wagon bed and chewed some cold corn tortillas that a woman had given us back in town.

"Tomorrow we'll be there," Josh announced. "I don't know whether to be happy about it or not. Hasn't been so bad, this trip."

"Yes, it has," I said, finishing my tortilla. "I've never been so tired. Every bit of me aches, and I'm starved half to death."

"And tomorrow you'll be just as tired, just as hungry, and we won't have anything important left to do."

"We'll have five days of hard traveling left before we get home."

"I don't think I'm going back, Jeff."

"What?"

"You've been up the road. Take one of the horses and ride home. Shouldn't be too hard."

"Josh?"

"I can shoot a rifle. I shot my first deer when I was only 11. I'm a better rider than any of my brothers. I ought to stay at Goliad with the army. I'd be some use there."

I took a deep breath and let it out slowly. It was hard to say what I was feeling. It was harder to confess how helpless I felt.

"I can't get back on my own, Josh," I finally admitted. "I can hardly stay on a horse 10 feet. I've never shot any deer."

"We'll figure out something, Jeff. Don't worry."

"It's hard not to worry," I said, shivering as the wind picked up. "We don't even know if they're still there. In Goliad. Or where the Mexicans are. Josh, aren't you a little bit afraid?"

"No," he insisted. "Pa and my brothers will be up there. Everything will be fine."

I hoped he was right, but I wasn't sure of anything. We slept side-by-side in the wagon that night, half-frozen and wondering what we would find tomorrow. Eventually even the cold couldn't keep me awake. The weariness overtook me, and I fell asleep.

It wasn't a peaceful night, though. My dreams were full of Mexican cavalry and blazing cannons. Three times I awoke screaming. Josh shook me clear of my nightmares, but we were both too tired to talk about them.

My last dream was the worst. I found myself lost and alone in the middle of nowhere. I had lost my horse, and I could hear people shouting from the underbrush, firing shots, and searching for me. All I could do was cover my ears and cry to myself. I was whimpering when Josh shook me awake.

"Sun's up," he announced. "Thought I'd fry us some eggs and a slice of bacon. How's that sound?"

"We ought to get started," I said, yawning away my weariness.

"We will. You go tend to the horses while I cook breakfast. You may not have as good a cook tomorrow."

"You still bound to join the army, Josh?"

"I am."

"Then I won't have as good a friend tomorrow, either," I told him.

# Chapter 4

## Los Tejanos

We forded two creeks on our way to Goliad. I was nervous the whole time, expecting Mexican cavalry to appear at any moment. In truth, all we saw was a hawk turning wide circles in the sky overhead and a couple of rabbits hopping alongside the road. That was fine by me.

"I thought you said we were just a few miles away!" I finally exclaimed. "We should have been there by now, Josh!"

"I was only guessing," he answered. "I only know what I've seen on maps."

"Is this the map in your head—the one I can't see?" I asked. "You sure we're not lost?"

"I'm not sure of anything," he admitted. "There aren't 20 roads from Victoria Guadalupe to La Bahia, though. We're going the right way."

"This is a road?" I asked. It was getting muddier and

muddier. I had scarcely uttered the words when the left back wheel struck a buried rock. You could hear the splintering of spokes a hundred yards away. Josh jumped off the wagon, landing with a splatter. I could tell from his silence that things were bad.

"Whoa," I called to the horses. They continued to try to pull the damaged wagon onward, and we turned sideways, sinking into the ruts of the road.

"Tie them off and come down here," Josh called. "We've got big trouble."

I did as told and joined him. The turning had separated five spokes from the wheel hub, and the corner of the wagon was sinking at a dangerous angle. Then the wheel collapsed entirely.

"To have come so far!" I shouted, kicking a stone down the road. "This far. This close. For what?"

Josh tried to pull me over, but I was too mad just then to be around anybody. I stormed out through the mud and up onto a slight rise of ground. Prairie grass covered the knoll, and at least I could kick away some of the dirt. Then I heard it—the sound of horses.

"Josh!" I called. "Someone's coming!"

"Get down here!" he shouted. "It could be Mexican cavalry!"

"I thought you said—"

"Never mind what I said," he told me as he fumbled around in the back of the wagon. He finally located his rifle and busied himself loading it. I didn't see how a couple of boys were going to fight off any Mexican cavalry, though, so I stayed right where I was. When a pair of riders appeared a few hundred feet off, I waved to them.

"Here!" I called. "Over here!"

"Jeff, you fool!" Josh barked. "You don't know who they are. Get over here and stay quiet."

"I haven't dragged these fool supplies halfway across the country to let 'em rot on this road," I replied. "Anyhow, they don't look like soldiers to me."

In truth, they weren't as old as we were. The oldest one approached us cautiously and stared hard into my eyes. I didn't know if he was Mexican or not. He was a little darker than I was, but I'd seen plenty of boys back in the Carolinas with brown eyes and dark hair. My own hair wasn't much lighter than his.

"Our wagon broke down," I explained, pointing down toward the road. "We're headed for Goliad."

"Americans?" he asked in an accented voice.

"Texians," Josh answered as he approached, rifle in hand. "You speak English?"

"Probably better than you speak Spanish," the taller one said, dismounting to have a closer look at the wheel. "I am Miguel Espinosa," he added. "This is my brother Pablo. Our rancho is nearby. You go to help the soldiers at the presidio?"

Josh motioned for me to keep silent, but I couldn't see how we were going to accomplish much by keeping mum.

"We're bringing supplies," I told the Espinosa brothers. "Our pas are in the army."

"Army?" Miguel said, laughing. "It's not much of an army. They will welcome your supplies, though. Come,

**36**

we'll take you to see our grandmother. She can maybe offer you a wagon."

"Our horses—" Josh objected.

"Leave them to us," Miguel urged. "They will be provided for."

Miguel extended his hand toward Josh, who shook it reluctantly. I shook the offered hand eagerly. I was glad for the help, and I imagined that if the Espinosas meant us harm they could have ridden off and brought somebody older to deal with us.

Their rancho was only a quarter-mile away, and we arrived there shortly. Actually, Miguel offered to let us ride, but Josh wouldn't have it. He continued to eye our rescuers cautiously.

"You're city-raised and used to strangers," Josh told me as we walked. "Me, I prefer to wait and see what lies ahead. These Tejanos may be on our side, but it's odd that they speak such good English."

"It's not odd," I argued. "It's lucky. I don't know but a handful of Spanish words myself. Pa tried to teach me some Spanish when we got to Mobile, but I've forgotten most of it."

"Wish I knew what they were saying," Josh grumbled.

I just laughed. "Wouldn't matter what language they're speaking, far behind as we are. Come on, let's catch up."

Despite Josh's suspicions, we arrived at Rancho Espinosa unharmed. Josh remained outside an arched entryway while I trotted after Miguel and Pablo to help them tend their horses. At the stable we were greeted by

three men who quickly took over the chore. Miguel spoke
only Spanish to them, and I understood very little of it. I
guessed it was about Josh and me, though. As deserted as
that stretch of Texas appeared, I didn't suppose they had a
lot of visitors.

Miguel finally turned back to me, but Pablo rushed off
on some other errand. In short order, I was led inside the
house and into a small parlor. There, a gray-haired woman
wearing a simple cotton dress greeted me warmly. Before I
quite knew what was happening, she had both of her arms
wrapped tightly around me and was hugging me to within
an inch of my life.

"My grandmother, Magdalena Espinosa," Miguel
explained.

"I'm delighted to meet you, ma'am," I said, bowing
slightly the way Pa had taught me.

"Southern manners," she said in perfect English.
"Miguel, tell Carmen to find some refreshment for our
guests. Now, young man, tell me what has brought you so
far from home."

I felt a little awkward trying to explain what I didn't
completely understand myself. She soon took over the
conversation, though, and I found myself sitting in a
heavy oak chair, sipping tea, and listening. It turned out
that Señora Espinosa had been born in New Orleans when
it was part of Spain. She had married a colonel in the
Spanish army and had come out to Goliad when the little
town renamed itself after Mexico's revolt against Spanish
rule. Her husband had died, but her son had taken over

the rancho, and the family was doing quite well for itself, owning hundreds of horses and cattle. Miguel's mother, Maria Espinosa, ran a small tavern in town.

By the time Señora Espinosa had finished speaking, Pablo appeared with Josh, and we were led into a dining room, where we were treated to thick broiled steaks and a spicy dish that reminded me of Ma's summer squash.

"They took my rifle," Josh whispered when he passed me a piece of pecan pie. "I don't like this, Jeff."

"If this is how they treat prisoners, I'd hate to think of what they do when friends arrive," I told him.

The Espinosas had a bigger surprise for us later that afternoon. Two men appeared with a cart drawn by oxen. Inside were the precious supplies bound for the presidio. A third man led Josh's four horses.

"We need to get the supplies to the men at the fort," I explained. "They are desperate. Close to starving."

"They manage to survive," Miguel said. For the first time I noticed a trace of anger in his voice.

"Be civil," his grandmother urged. Turning back to Josh and me, she said, "You boys must understand that not everyone is glad that the Americans have come to La Bahia. In the past, Americans took the fort and fought Spanish troops. Our people are always the ones who suffer. Both armies come and take what they want.
They leave behind poverty and disease."

"But I thought it was the Texians, all of them, fighting for independence," I said. "Back in Mobile—"

"Yes, I lived for a time in New Orleans after President

Jefferson purchased the Louisiana country from the French," Señora Espinosa said, smiling. "There is some truth, but only some, in what you have heard. The new presidente, Santa Anna, is not a man much bothered by the Constitution. But if no one had fired on his soldiers, he would have found, as the Spanish did, that *Tejas* is too far away and too small to be a threat to his authority. These Americans who have come and captured his garrisons have changed all that. That is why he's come to our country."

Josh, who hadn't been listening to the rest, heard *that*.

"He's here?" Josh asked. "The army's really in Texas?"

"We have heard that there are already soldiers in Bexar," Miguel added. "An army is only a few days from here. I speak with my friends. They say a regiment of cavalry, perhaps a thousand men, have been sent to capture the presidio. El Presidente has maybe three thousand more with him."

"That's a lot of men," I said, eyeing Josh. "Maybe too many."

"Reinforcements are coming, though," Josh insisted. "Wait and see."

"Will they do us any good here?" I asked, anxiously gazing at the ox cart. "Josh?"

"It's not something boys should worry about," Señora Espinosa argued. "What will happen, will happen. It's in God's hands." She crossed herself and then motioned to one of her men. He mounted a horse and set off westward.

"He goes to tell Colonel Fannin at La Bahia of the

**40**

supplies," Miguel explained. "Soon he will send men to bring you to the presidio."

"Can't we just take the supplies ourselves?" I asked. "Who's Fannin anyway?"

"Colonel James Walker Fannin, Jr.," Josh said, looking at me as if I'd just asked the most idiotic question imaginable. "He commands this whole wing of the army."

"And how was I to know that?" I cried.

"Calm yourselves," Señora Espinosa pleaded. "Darkness comes early now. Let the colonel send you an escort in the morning. It's best that way. Not all of our neighbors are kind to strangers."

I nodded nervously.

"Maybe I can have my rifle back then," Josh suggested.

"It will be returned when you leave my protection," Señora Espinosa replied. "Here, you are safe."

I learned more about the history of Texas in the one day that we spent at the rancho than in all the time I'd spent in Mr. Peterson's school. It seemed that, years before, when the United States wasn't even a country, the Spanish had settled in Texas. The first settlers were priests, who built missions to convert the Indians and teach them farming. They had brought Spanish cattle with them too, which spread across the open range like wildfire. Miguel told me that most of the time the missions didn't have any sort of idea how large those herds were. Now the ranchers marked their animals with brands, but an awful lot of cattle still strayed northwestward. It was the same with horses. Texas was full of wandering herds, and Miguel's own grandfather had built up his holdings by chasing down the unbranded creatures and taking them for his own.

"American men see all this land and think they can come here and take it," Miguel told me. "They have come often. Sometimes the Mexican army has driven them away, but a few always remain. We Tejanos have stayed close to our settlements because of trouble with Indians. When our nation came into being, we thought that offering land to settlers who would come and populate the territory was a good idea. So we have Americans like Austin. Irishmen and Germans too. They were supposed to adopt our language and religion, but they didn't. Now it is they, not us, who rebel."

"Then why are you helping us?"

"Yes, I know it seems odd," he said, laughing. "Do you know that, here in Goliad, a resolution was passed for an independent Texas? This happened, but then some of the old people said we should not break away. Many Tejanos would not join a rebellion against their mother country. Some continue to feel that way. My father is a man of the law—a judge, you would call him. Because he is not a supporter of Santa Anna, he is a judge no longer."

"Where's your father now?" I asked.

"It's difficult to know," Miguel said, staring southward. "In January he left to purchase a bull. We have no letters from him. Maybe he is arrested. Who can say?"

"My pa's supposed to be at the fort," I said, sighing. "I guess we both wonder, huh?"

"I don't think this will be a good time for either of us, amigo. A thousand cavalry? These are the best soldiers in all of Mexico. Too many, I think, for Fannin. Too many, perhaps, for all the men in Texas to fight."

"And thousands more elsewhere?" I asked.

"Of course, these may be only words," Miguel said, forcing a smile. "It's a long way to Texas, and the winter has been hard. Perhaps these soldiers have suffered along the way."

"Maybe there are only nine hundred now."

"Maybe," he said, matching my dark gaze. "I think perhaps you should stay here when the soldiers come to get the cart."

"I have letters for my pa," I explained. "I want to see him too. Afterward, I plan to head back to Columbia."

"Is that your home?" Miguel asked.

"I don't know," I said. "It was a few days ago. Won't mean much without Pa, though."

"I understand those words," Miguel said, gripping my hands in his own. "That, if nothing else, makes us brothers."

Josh and I slept on our blankets beside the ox cart that night. Señora Espinosa had invited us inside, and Miguel had offered us his room. But Josh insisted that we had our duty to the supplies, and I decided I couldn't leave him out there alone. We didn't say much to each other. Weary though I was, I couldn't seem to get to sleep. Eventually I took a walk and stared up at the sky. Clouds had swallowed the stars, so I couldn't tell if Pa's comet was up there. I hoped it was.

I finally faded off into a light sleep, but a thousand Mexican horsemen rode through my dreams, and I found no peace. Not long after dawn, the sound of horses' hooves brought me to my feet. A handful of riders dressed in every kind of outfit imaginable galloped toward us, led by a young girl.

"Carlita!" I heard Pablo shout from the house. Soon he and Miguel were rushing out to greet the girl, who I guessed was their older sister. Among the other riders was a trio of red-haired fellows—and Pa!

I'm not sure what I yelled to him, but he was off his horse and waiting with outstretched arms when I reached him. He lifted me up off the ground a moment before setting me back down.

"Jefferson, you've gone and grown old on me," he declared, pretending pain.

"I'm not so old as all that," I said, handing over Ma's letters. "We've missed you past measuring."

"As I have you, son," he declared as he opened the first letter. "Got a house built, it says! How did you manage that?"

I started explaining. Josh was no doubt doing much the same. His pa and brothers seemed every inch as glad to see him.

"Sergeant, don't you think we ought to get these supplies headed for the fort?" a sandy-haired fellow no more than 17 asked.

"There's time," Pa replied. "Andrew, this here's my oldest boy," he added. "Jefferson, this youngster is Andrew

Case of the New Orleans Grays. If he seems fretful, it's
because he's got an older brother at the Alamo."

"The Alamo's our fort in San Antonio," Andrew
explained. "They're under attack there by thousands of
Mexicans, and Colonel Fannin hasn't lifted a finger to
help."

"We made one try," Pa told me. "Truth is, Fannin's
made a muddle of everything. I confess the supplies are
welcome, and I'm glad to see you, son. Even so, I wish you
were a thousand miles from the trouble that's brewing
hereabouts."

"I heard about Mexican cavalry," I told him. "Miguel
says there might be a thousand of them headed this way."

"Well, son, I wish the Mexican army was the only
problem we had," Pa told me as he led the way back to his
horse. Already Josh's brother Seth had taken charge of the
four horses Josh had brought out. Carla was issuing orders
to bring out oxen to haul the cart.

"That would seem trouble enough," I remarked.

"Is," Pa agreed, "for most folks, anyway."

"Pa, I've been having bad dreams lately. I've—"

"Never you mind about that now, son," he answered.
"All will be better now that I'm with you."

# Chapter 5

## Fort Defiance

Josh let go a powerful curse when he found out we were only six miles from Goliad. Me, I was just glad we'd gotten the supplies to Colonel Fannin's men and found our fathers. After almost a week on my own, I was glad to have somebody else deciding things.

I sat in the ox cart with the provisions as we headed for the fort. That very morning I got my first look at the old Spanish presidio that the Texians had renamed Fort Defiance. It wasn't half as grand as the forts at Charleston or the great walled structures guarding the entrance to Mobile Bay. To be truthful, it didn't seem like a real fort at all. The northeast corner was a church! And the walls didn't seem high enough to keep out a determined enemy.

Once inside, I saw how wrong I had been. The gates were sturdy, and the walls proved deceptively high—10 feet in places. They were close to three feet thick too. The walls were pierced in places with firing positions, and these in turn were narrowed so that shots could get out but not in. The real advantage of the place was that it stood on high ground. Except for the ruins of a few buildings outside the walls, the garrison had clear fields of fire against any attacker. There were captured cannons mounted here and there, and across from the church was a stone barracks used to house the men. The three acres inside were covered with prairie grass, and a well provided fresh water.

"So long as the enemy doesn't bring heavy guns, we're halfway safe," Pa assured me. "Of course, we wouldn't turn away a little more food or some reinforcements."

Colonel Fannin had the men busy strengthening the walls when we arrived, but he came over to personally thank Josh and me for our help.

"You boys have provided a badly needed lift," he declared. "It probably would be best, though, if you started making your way back home as soon as possible. Our spies tell us that the enemy may be nearby."

I shuddered.

Josh grunted and stared at his father. "I'm going nowhere," he declared. "You'll find I can shoot straight enough. There are already three Saglers here. Might as well make it four."

"Glad to have you, little brother," Sam replied.

Their father shook his head.

"I think you would be more use at home, helping your

ma," Mr. Sagler argued. "Josh, I don't expect us to run into any trouble so big that we can't handle it with the men already here."

The colonel started to speak, but a glare from Josh's pa stopped him. Truth be told, there were plenty of boys no older than 15 in the garrison. Far too many of them, according to Pa.

"In a real fight, these children are going to fall apart," he told me later. "I feel like I'm a nursemaid half the time."

"I heard that," Andrew said, grinning. "He's giving you the talk about who has chin whiskers, is he? Well, ask him who's been out there scouting the enemy. Who's been carrying dispatches, Sergeant?"

"He rides almost as well as he talks," Pa told me. "He thinks that because he rode down to Guadalupe Victoria last week, he passes for a courier."

"Where's the lieutenant from Mobile?" I asked, glancing around at the three or four hundred men in the fort. "You know, the lawyer from Montgomery."

"Lieutenant Bonham's been down to ask for reinforcements," Pa told me. "He and most of the New Orleans boys are up in San Antonio."

"There's been talk that the Mexican army is up there," I said, frowning. "I don't expect it's true, but—"

"It's true," Andrew declared, glancing warily toward the north. "We started up that way to join Travis, but we got some wagons stuck crossing the river. I don't think the colonel had his heart in it anyway."

"Your brother's there?" I asked.

"He'll give a fair account of himself," Andrew boasted. "Just the same, I wish the rest of us were there to help."

"Be best if we were all together," Pa agreed, "but we aren't. Besides, any fool can see that we can't leave the way open along the coast for the Mexicans to flank us. It will take a fair number of soldiers to take this fort."

"Pa, I've been up that road, and there isn't all that much to it. Won't we be in a box if the Mexicans come down from the north and cut us off?"

"Son, we'd best talk a bit," he said, leading me away from the others. "Jefferson, I'm a sergeant and I'm expected to follow orders. If I wasn't, I'd throw you over the first horse in sight, grab another for myself, and head fast as lightning back to Alabama. This business has been mishandled from the first. Fannin's sent men off here and there, and he had the bulk of us headed up the road to San Antonio with no scouts. He tells us he's West Point trained, but as I hear it, they booted him out. He's a brave man, but he's in over his head and drowning fast. I'd follow him in a charge, son, but I hate to think of him planning how to fight this war. He's sure to get a lot of good men killed."

It didn't exactly cheer me to see Pa so down on the colonel, and a lot of the men were grumbling even louder. The New Orleans boys were worried about their friends fighting in the old mission up north, and some of the rest wanted to join the men down at Refugio, who were supposed to be marching toward Mexico. Other groups were off at this place and that, but none of the towns meant anything to me.

Turning my thoughts to the Espinosas, I did feel obliged to return the ox cart to them.

"No need to go back to their place," Andrew told me. "When she's not riding around on her horse, Carla works at her mother's tavern. She's got a brother with her. Let him take the cart home."

I started to argue, but Pa waved me silent.

"Andrew, you show the boy where the cantina is. You can lead oxen, can't you, Jefferson?"

"Yes, sir," I said, not entirely convinced of it.

"I'll lend a hand," Josh volunteered.

So with Andrew and Josh leading the oxen, and me mainly trailing behind, we made our way into Goliad proper. According to Andrew, it had been a town of better than 500 people before the latest fighting broke out. Now most of the people had fled to their ranchos or gone south to stay with relatives. Most of those who remained eyed us suspiciously. Only a few greeted us. Among those was a tall woman in her late thirties, Maria Espinosa.

"Ah, my lovely oxen!" she exclaimed as we approached the small cantina she operated with her two oldest children. "And which of you are the brave boys who brought the food from the Rio Brazos?"

"Josh and I, ma'am," I said, bowing to her and motioning to Josh.

"And Andrew comes along to keep Carla from her work," Señora Espinosa said, laughing as she took charge of the beasts. "Hernando, come and see what's arrived."

A slender boy about five and a half feet tall trotted out the cantina door. Except for the faint start of a moustache, he looked exactly like his younger brothers. He ignored us and inspected the cart.

"They've done it no harm, Madre," he finally observed. "Should I take it back to the rancho?"

"That would be best," Señora Espinosa replied. " 'Nando, I think you should stay there for a time. If the soldiers are really coming, your grandmother will welcome your help."

"The soldiers are already here," he growled, waving his arms toward us.

"These ones?" she asked, grinning. "They are no army. When you see the Mexican army, then you will know what soldiers are."

I thought that maybe Andrew would protest, but he remained silent. Señora Espinosa waved us toward the cantina doors, and Andrew led us inside. He and Josh headed over to where a dark-haired girl about my age was cleaning the tables. I found myself facing Señora Espinosa alone.

"So," she said, giving me a motherly look that was a mixture of scolding and pleading, "now you will go home?"

"If I can," I answered. "Josh is talking of staying with the army, though, and the wagon broke down."

"Our men at the rancho will fix it. You will go back then?"

I tried to avoid her intense gaze. It wasn't possible.

"Ma'am, the thing is, I can't ride a horse worth a penny. I'm no good at handling animals. I don't know my way, and I'd probably just end up lost and alone."

"You could follow the couriers to Victoria Guadalupe," she suggested. "Someone might take you home from there."

"Nobody's going to take a fool boy like me anywhere," I said, dropping my eyes. "I'm hoping Pa will take me back himself. He's tired of soldiering."

"Your father won't leave," she said, smoothing out my hair. "My father was a soldier. I know how it is, you see. I have met the sergeant. He is one of the few who wears a uniform. There are some like him here, and that's good. When it comes time for fighting, he will be a rock. The others, well, they don't have the heart for it. Too many are just here for the land. They have no courage. And so many are young."

"Do you have to be old to have courage?"

"Not always," she said, grinning at me. She kissed my forehead and poured me a glass of cool water. "Courage can get a boy killed, though. I know. I had three brothers. They, too, were soldiers. The Spanish killed the oldest. The others—well, we've had many revolutions since Mexico became a nation. I came here to escape the fighting, but it has followed me."

I nodded. She kissed my forehead again, and I was reminded of the time Ma took me in her arms after Grandpa Henry left us. Part of me longed for that comfort, but I could see Josh and Andrew staring. I stiffened my back and steadied my nerves. "I'll see about getting home," I declared, "but if it doesn't work out, I'll stick to Pa. We'll make our stand together."

"Don't be too eager to die," she pleaded. "There will be enough killing."

It was only later, when Andrew and Josh introduced me to Carla, that I learned why the señora seemed so troubled about me getting home.

"When you were at my home, did you visit my father's study?" Carla asked.

"No," I told her. "I was mainly in the parlor and the kitchen."

"The dining room," she said, correcting me. "Grandmother would never allow a guest in the kitchen. On my grandfather's desk, the one Padre uses, is a portrait of my Uncle Roberto. He was Grandfather's aide when they drove the Spaniards from Vera Cruz. It was Uncle Roberto who introduced my parents. Poor Roberto had little luck, though. He died in his first battle. Except for your eyes, you look very much like him."

"I'm not even 14," I told her. "Your uncle must have been a lot older."

"Oh, much older," she agreed. "He was 15. He got no older. I heard you talking. Perhaps you could go to the rancho and wait to see what happens. If El Presidente is defeated, you can rejoin your father. If Colonel Fannin loses, though, you could stay at the rancho. Madre would be happy to look after you."

"And you? Would you be happy?" Josh asked.

"With so many brothers, would I notice another one?" she asked.

"Maybe I could go there too," Andrew suggested.

"I wouldn't mind, either," Josh added.

"You both can ride horses," Carla barked, "and you are old enough to display better manners. Don't you have a fort to repair? Go on, all of you!"

She picked up a broom, and we vanished out the door. I could hear her laughter chasing us for better than a city block.

If we had been able to pass those next few days with Carla and her mother, my stay in Goliad wouldn't have been half bad. Instead, I joined Pa's working party and helped repair two gun carriages. Although Fort Defiance was well armed and nearly repaired, something or other was continually breaking.

March didn't prove a lucky time for the little Texian army. All of the news that arrived at Goliad seemed bad. First came word that the Matamoras force had been caught by General Jose Urrea's Mexican cavalry and cut to pieces. Colonel Fannin sent Andrew out to see if he could locate the former governor of Tennessee, General Sam Houston, who was supposed to be at Gonzales with an army of Texas settlers. The colonel also dispatched a company of men to the town of Refugio to bring a force of Texians occupying an old mission there safely to Goliad.

"Looks like we're finally going to have a fight on our hands," Josh told me. "What are you going to do, Jeff?

Stay here or hide out at Rancho Espinosa?"

"I suppose it's easier for you," I said, swallowing hard. "You know how to shoot and ride. Me, I've only hunted a few times, and I've never come close to fighting in a real battle. I'll be 14 before the month's out, though. I think I'm too young to do much good but too old to run away and hide."

"It'll be good to have you with us," Josh said, gripping my hand. "We'll be safe enough here in the fort."

But that proved to be the problem. After spending several weeks repairing and strengthening Fort Defiance, rumors that we were leaving the place began to spread. It didn't make sense. Then Andrew returned. A courier from General Houston was with him. One look at Andrew's face told me they weren't bringing good news. It wasn't long before the colonel summoned the officers to a meeting.

Pa shared the sad news with me. "It's as bad as it gets, Jefferson," he said, gripping my shoulders and pulling me close. "Santa Anna took the Alamo last Sunday. Everyone, the whole garrison, was put to the sword. Except for a few women and children, no one got away alive. It's feared that our men at Refugio are also lost. There may be four thousand Mexicans on their way here right now. General Houston's ordered us to blow up the fort and retreat to Guadalupe Victoria."

"How close are the Mexicans?" I asked.

"Andrew said that the road's clear behind us but it may not stay that way. We've got cannons to haul, ox carts to carry our provisions, and no horses to carry us. The closest

Mexicans are cavalry, and they can cover two miles while we march one. Son, I wish you had stayed in Columbia."

I couldn't tell him that I wished it too, for that wasn't true. If Pa was in trouble, I wanted to be with him, to help him. The problem was that I wasn't sure I could do anything helpful.

Andrew solved my problem for me. Maybe it was thinking about his brother dead in San Antonio that drew him closer to Pa and me. He didn't have any blood kin now. Anyway, he suggested I help the doctors. We had several with us, including a kind-hearted fellow from Illinois named Dr. Joe Barnard. He had enlisted as a lowly private, to hear him tell it, but he had become the command's chief surgeon. Andrew said Barnard was considering leaving, but I discovered otherwise.

"Way I see it, Jeff," he said, "I'll only be safe if these men are victorious. Fannin loses, and there won't be many Americans safe in Texas."

Some of the soldiers grumbled about retreating, especially the Louisiana boys whose friends had been killed at the Alamo. Most didn't see a lot of choice, especially after word reached us that the Refugio men had been caught and killed. By my tally, we'd lost 200 on the coast and almost that many with Travis in San Antonio. We 300 or so were all that remained of the whole army. But although the colonel had decided to leave Goliad, he seemed in no big hurry to get started.

One bunch of men was for heading out and leaving the cannons behind. "We can get horses at the ranchos and do some real damage," a big Georgian boasted. "We're better at fighting in the woods anyway. Only a fool fights out in the open, in neat lines."

"You plan to go chasing after a thousand Mexican cavalrymen?" Josh's brother Seth asked. "You'd leave our big guns behind too. You know just as much about soldiering as the colonel does."

A lot of the men were just plain nervous. Some turned glum, especially after a scouting party of Mexicans appeared within sight of the fort. We had about 30 mounted men of our own, and when they rode out, the Mexicans scattered. It proved mildly entertaining, the sort of seesaw affair that followed. Then a fair-sized force of Mexicans appeared, and our cavalry wound up trapped in the old Spanish mission across the river from Fort Defiance.

The Red Rovers, a company of about 70 Alabama boys, marched out to rescue the horsemen. The Mexicans put up only a half-hearted charge. There was some shooting, and our boys fired off a cannon. Then things got quiet again.

We cheered the Rovers and the cavalry when they returned. Still, knowing the enemy was close at hand wasn't much to warm you on a cool night.

"See?" the boastful Georgian declared afterward. "Told you they weren't so hot for a fight."

"Maybe not," one of the Rovers answered. "I'll fight if I have to, but if those Mexicans will leave me alone I'll head back to Alabama. Six hundred acres of land isn't worth dying over."

"I guess the price of land just went up," Andrew told me as he sat beside me at supper that night. "I should have gone ahead on my own when the colonel turned around. At least I might have died with Ben. It's hard facing your death with no kin close at hand."

I think he intended to cheer me, feeling Pa would be glad of my company. It didn't work that way, though.

As for Pa, he scribbled a letter to Ma and handed it to me. "There's a better chance of you getting home," he declared.

I wasn't half so sure. Except for the Espinosas and a few other Tejano families, the people seemed to have turned against us. Some of our soldiers had started taking things—food especially—from the town folk. The officers turned a blind eye to such doings.

"It's going to get worse," Pa told me. "Some of these men don't see that they've got much to lose now."

I couldn't help remembering the day that Pa and the rest of the Mobile Grays marched aboard their ship. Well, Lieutenant Bonham and many of those men were dead now. Pa and the few still alive didn't hold out a lot of hope for the future.

I was watching a group of artillerymen drag extra cannons out to the river when Josh found me the next day. They were sinking the guns that Pa and I had worked so hard to mount. We couldn't haul them with us, though, so we weren't going to leave anything behind that the enemy could use.

"Scared?" Josh asked as he sat beside me.

"Scared enough," I admitted. "I wish I'd learned to ride."

"It wouldn't have mattered," he told me. "You would have stuck by your pa, same as me. I don't know what dying's like, but I can't help but wonder. Our mothers have boys back home to help. We're old enough to do our part."

I wished I could have believed that, but a feeling of uselessness gnawed at me. Although I had my doubts, I was determined to take my place beside Dr. Barnard when we left Fort Defiance. Whatever lay ahead, I would do my best to help whenever I had the chance.

"It's all a man can do," Pa had told me once. I prayed I wouldn't come up short of the mark.

# Chapter 6

## Coleto Creek

We had seemed like a considerable force while manning the fort. When we took to the road that next day, though, we looked a pitifully weak army. We wasted most of the early morning cooking breakfast, and then we spent some more time burning provisions. I didn't understand military tactics, but when we started burning flour and salted pork—some of it brought out from Columbia by Josh and me—I couldn't conceal my anger. The men could have carried most of the food, and if we were gone long we'd miss it.

What was worse, any Mexican scout worth a penny could tell by the smoke that we were getting ready to leave. We were as much as inviting an attack. "Don't worry too much," Dr. Barnard said, shaking his head at the waste. "Our boys did well enough against those scouts. If worse comes to worst, we can split into bands and disperse into the woodlands."

The only trouble was that we weren't headed for a forest. As Josh and I knew, the country outside the fort was mostly prairie. That made good ground for cavalry and mighty poor cover for defense.

Colonel Fannin appeared unconcerned. I suppose he was as disappointed as anybody to abandon the fort he'd spent so much time and effort on, but he now convinced us that General Houston was at Guadalupe Victoria with an army waiting to support us.

"There's a lot of walking between here and there," Josh reminded me.

"And how much walking are you going to do?" I asked. "You've got your horses."

"Colonel Fannin wanted them for a wagon," Josh said, sighing. "Pa said we were infantry, anyhow."

We actually left the fort in fair humor, though. The little skirmish with the Mexicans had helped lift our spirits, and the Rovers actually sang as they marched. There was a good force of regular Texas soldiers among us, and they marched in a neat column. Before we got a mile outside Goliad, though, our little army was strung out all over the place. The cannons had already taken a bath crossing the San Antonio River outside the fort, and I knew there were at least two creeks close by to get across before we would finish our day's marching. Dr. Barnard traveled in a cart carrying three sick men. I marched alongside, climbing up to offer the sick men water from time to time. Otherwise I kept pace with the oxen's slow plodding.

Pa was with a mixed company of Mobile and New Orleans boys. He tried to keep some order in the ranks, but weeks confined in a fort didn't prepare them for the long march. Nearly everyone was wet from fording the river and a shallow creek farther along. A lot of the younger men grumbled about their ragged clothes. At least I had good shoes and a decent coat.

As it turned out, none of that mattered very much. Being at the rear of the column of marchers, I couldn't help noticing our cavalry riding past and looping around toward the west. "There!" one of the sick fellows shouted, pointing his weary arm in the same direction. It was as if the whole horizon was a sea of Mexicans. I noticed that our men had quickened their pace. Andrew took a stick and whacked the oxen, hoping they would hurry along, but it did no good. They were taking their own sweet time.

I glanced back from time to time at the Mexicans behind us. Even a city boy could tell they were getting closer. There were cavalry moving along our flanks too, and Colonel Fannin rode along the line, shouting at us to hurry the carts along. The cannons were also falling behind. Finally officers began pulling their companies off here and there while we moved on down the road to a slight rise. Just ahead lay the second creek and some trees that promised cover. We never got that far.

The Mexican commander, General Urrea, had foxed us

proper. He'd managed to get another company of
horsemen around and ahead of us. Colonel Fannin
decided it was time to organize a defense. Against all
argument, he began forming us into a square.

"It's the best way to stop a cavalry charge," Dr. Barnard
told me.

But there was higher ground around us, and we had no
escape route. Without food and having only the water in
our canteens, we couldn't hold out long in the open. For
the colonel, leaving the cannons and the sick behind was
unthinkable, though. So it was decided to form our lines
there on the prairie and leave our fate to the Almighty.

Despite all the tales of fighting that Grandpa Henry
and Pa had shared over the years, I was unprepared for the
battle's opening shots. They came from a party of Mexican
horsemen. Our own cavalry had already forded the creek
and had set off to scout the road ahead. Now they were
trying to return. It was difficult to see anything clearly.
The muddy ruts that had passed for a road two weeks
earlier had become a world of dust, and the horses raised a
cloud of the stuff with their trampling hooves. Powder
smoke mixed in, and we could determine nothing about
the fighting.

"Never you mind about it," Dr. Barnard told me as he
fought to maintain control of the oxen. "Help with the
cart."

I took one step toward the oxen, but strong hands
grabbed me and held me in place. It was Andrew Case.
"Watch," he said, moving forward with a blanket. He

threw it over the frightened animals, covering their eyes. With the help of a half-dozen artillerymen, we got the cart within the square and released the oxen. Quick as they shed the blanket, they moved off toward the creek.

The horses and oxen hauling our cannons fared little better. They either broke away and headed for the water or turned toward the Mexicans. Those that remained with us soon fell victim to the brave Mexican sharpshooters who made a rush forward, got within range, and did their deadly work quickly. Our own rifles barked a sharp reply, and only a few of the enemy marksmen escaped with their lives.

"Did the job, though," Andrew grumbled as he helped me carry the sick men to cover. "If we try to break their line now, we'll have to leave the guns behind."

I nodded my understanding. Those Mexicans were putting us in a real fix, but when they formed up and charged our line, they got a proper peppering of lead. Our cannons did some serious work too, blasting gaps in the disciplined Mexican line. The cries of the wounded and dying tormented my ears, and I found myself shivering beside the cart. "Enough of that, Jeff," Dr. Barnard scolded me. "See if you can find some water for the wounded."

I glanced over to my right and saw Seth Sagler lying on a blanket, bleeding from a hole in his right arm. I felt my knees wobble, but I steadied myself. I dashed over to the supply carts, but apparently all our water jugs were in a cart 20 feet outside the square. Its oxen lay dead, and there was little hope of dragging it any closer.

"You didn't want to live forever, did you?" a familiar voice asked.

I turned and looked into Josh's eyes.

"I was hoping to make it to 14," I told him.

We weren't the first to try for the water, though. Two Georgians leaped out from the front rank and raced toward the cart. One got halfway before the Mexicans unleashed a volley. Three musket balls hit his body and ripped the life out of him. The other fellow reached the cart, grabbed a jug, and raced back safely.

"Our turn," Josh said, taking a deep breath. I nodded. We then crept forward.

"Hold up a minute," a tall young Tejano called from behind one of our cannons. He was one of the men who had joined us from the original presidio: our best gunner. I regret not knowing his name because he was killed before the hour was up. With the help of the Rovers, he managed to turn the gun toward the Mexican lines and get it loaded. It went off with a boom, and the first file of enemy soldiers opposite the cart screamed in terror.

I leaped out from our line and ran as fast as I could to the cart. When I was five feet away, I dove under the big wooden wheel on the right side. Mexican riflemen tore splinters from the cart and the wheel, but they missed me. After they finished, I climbed in and picked up a jug in each arm. Then, as the cannon fired its second round, I dashed back to our line.

The men shouted and slapped my back, but I didn't see Josh. Turning back, I retraced my steps with my eyes.

Just to the right of the oxen lay a dark shape. It took a minute or two to sink in. The Mexicans hadn't missed entirely.

"Here," I said, handing over the jugs and pointing to Dr. Barnard. I then took a deep breath and turned back toward the cart. This time I raced out on my own. Mexican shots peppered the ground near the cart, but except for losing a piece out of the heel of my shoe, I reached Josh unhurt. I grabbed his shoulders and pulled him under the cart with me. His eyes were already glassy, though, and his whole shirt was soaked with blood.

"Tell Pa—" he began to mutter. It was all he could say, though. He died right there in my arms.

I wanted to stay there, to grieve for my dead friend, but the firing was getting heavier. The Mexicans were bringing their own cannons into action too, and one threw a big round ball into the earth not 10 yards from the cart.

I knew that the water was the most important thing to the unit, so I climbed up into the wagon, wrapped five jugs in a blanket, and started to heave them over the side. I couldn't manage the weight, so I removed one. Then I rolled the blanket over the side and leaped after it. As I landed, a cannon ball struck close by, upending the cart. Amid the shower of rock and dust, I grabbed the blanket and headed back to our lines.

I couldn't move very fast with such a heavy load, but two of our cannons opened fire on the Mexican battery. The soldiers who might have fired at me had their heads down, and so I managed to drag myself to safety. It was only after reaching Dr. Barnard and the other surgeons that I collapsed.

"Jeff?" Andrew called to me.

I managed to wipe my eyes on my shirtsleeve before looking up.

"I'm all right," I told him.

"Not entirely," he said, dabbing my left shoulder with a strip of cloth. I felt a sharp sting, and he showed me where a Mexican musket ball had taken a slice out of my upper left arm. I looked the rest of myself over, but except for a tear in the left knee of my trousers, I appeared in one piece.

"That was a fool thing you did," the doctor said, binding my wound. "It's a miracle you're still alive."

"You needed water," I said, trembling as I tried to erase the look of Josh's torn body from my memory.

"Well, we have enough for now. You sit here and rest."

The battle started an hour or so past midday and went on till sundown. I spent a time recovering my wits, but eventually I helped tend the wounded. I did my best to cheer Seth, but he faded off as the sun set.

I then made my way to where Pa and the other Mobile boys were manning their part of the square. Like most of the men, they were scratching a ditch out of the hard ground and throwing up every odd bit of brush, dead animals, sacks, or saddles in sight in order to offer some protection against the coming assault.

"I should've learned to ride," I said, settling in

alongside Pa.

"Looks as if you had a bit of adventure," he said, examining my arm. "Good thing you haven't grown any taller."

"Haven't gotten any smarter, Pa. That's for sure. Josh's dead."

"That's a real shame," Pa said, wrapping his arm around me. "Jefferson, he was a fine young man. I read your ma's account of how he helped build our house. I understand he had a brother hit too."

"Seth," I said, shaking off the tears forming in my eyes. "He's dead too."

"We've lost a few here and there, but we've kept the enemy at bay. The colonel's not much on making decisions, but he's a dandy in a fight."

I nodded my agreement. Colonel Fannin had been hit too, in his side just above the hip. He had ignored the pain and limped around, shouting encouragement and cheering the good work done by our rifles. We could see the fires of the enemy all around us, though, and the voices of their singing carried into our camp. We also could smell the aromas drifting from their cooking fires. I hadn't eaten anything since breakfast, and I'd only had two sips of water to drink. The day had been hot for March, and it wasn't likely to get better come dawn.

"Keep alert, men," Colonel Fannin urged as he made his final inspection of the lines that night. "Keep a guard awake. They may try to rush us at dawn."

"If they do, they'll need a lot of coffins," someone called.

I suppose it was remarkable. Desperate as we were, most of the men seemed happier than they had been in weeks.

"It's why they came here," Pa explained. "They understand fighting. It's hiding in forts or running away that baffles them."

"I suppose," I told him. "I do wish we'd reached the creek, though. I'm awful thirsty."

"I know, son," he said, studying my eyes. He passed me his canteen, but I shook my head.

"Best we save the water for the wounded," I told him.

"You are one of the wounded," he said, lifting my chin. I tasted the water, but I refused to take more than a swallow. I was no worse off than most of the army, and come daybreak it would be more important for the men with rifles to be fit for action.

That night the Mexicans blew their bugles from time to time, startling us from our sleep. Between those horns and the moans of our 50 or so wounded, it was hard to sleep. One of the officers suggested trying to break through the Mexican line and reach the creek, but it meant abandoning our cannons and wounded. There were about 250 men fit enough to make the try, and Colonel Fannin estimated the enemy at close to 2,000 men. We had killed a few of them, but they were sure to have the escape path toward Guadalupe Victoria blocked. Besides, most of their army was cavalry and they wouldn't have had a difficult time running us down. If we were forced to make a desperate fight, why abandon men who had served so bravely?

Our sole hope was that our cavalry had reached help. It was a slim chance at best.

Dawn broke the next morning, chasing a heavy mist from the prairie. Pa roused me out of a deep sleep. It surprised me that with all the ruckus going on, I had managed to drift off. For once I'd had no nightmares—at least not in my sleep. The Mexicans fired two heavy chains from their cannons, and they made a terrifying sound as they whirled over our heads. Neither did any harm, though, and moments later an officer stepped out of their ranks carrying a white flag.

"I guess they're going to surrender, huh?" Andrew asked as he helped me to my feet. "Doc Barnard needs your help, Jeff."

"Pa?" I asked. If a final fight was coming, I preferred to stay where I was.

"You'll do more good with the surgeons," Pa declared. "They've had a hard time of it, I'm sure."

I nodded my agreement and followed Andrew to where the doctors were stationed. I didn't know much about medicine, but the men seemed to like having me with them. Some would talk about their sons or younger brothers back home. Others asked if I would write a few lines to wives or mothers or sweethearts. I did what I could, but we soon ran short of paper.

Eventually Colonel Fannin had decided to treat with General Urrea and agreed on terms. Word had it that we would give up our arms, march back to Goliad, and wait for a ship to carry us to New Orleans. This suited a fair number of the men, but the Rovers and the men with Pa argued for fighting on. Both had heard that prisoners taken at Refugio had been killed. Myself, I'd found the Espinosas honorable folks and expected the Mexicans would keep their word. It seemed that they'd fought us bravely enough, after all. If they meant to kill us all, why not just resume their cannon fire and leave us to starve?

Naturally, nobody asked me my opinion. Nor were the soldiers consulted. For once Colonel Fannin made a decision on his own. He came back from the parley and told us we were surrendered. Some of the Rovers busted their rifles when they got the news. There was more talk of breaking away.

"Boys, they'll kill everyone who doesn't get away," Pa told his little circle of men. Other officers said the same thing. Considerable shouting and cursing ensued, but nobody fired a shot at the Mexicans. The battle was over.

The Mexican troops handled the surrender with a kind of precision that left me feeling at ease. Each of our men stepped up and gave his name, stacked his gun, turned over his personal property in another stack, and moved on. The Mexicans themselves were in a fine mood, smoking cigars and babbling away. One or two even came over to me and looked at my bandage. They made shooting motions with their hands, and I could tell they remembered my run for the water jugs.

The real surprise was the sight of Hernando Espinosa dressed in the uniform of a Mexican bugler. He did his best to ignore me, but when a private shoved me toward the road, he barked angrily at the man.

# Chapter 7

## Medicos

The surrender went well enough. Afterward, though, the grass caught fire, and the wagon holding all our powder and ammunition exploded. Wood splinters showered the prairie, and the Mexicans accused us of setting it on fire. We should have, I suppose, but in truth the only ones hurt were our own men. Two were burned badly, and several others were hurt by splinters.

One thing I didn't understand about our treatment was the order to march back to Goliad immediately. We had neither eaten nor drunk anything in well past a day, and suddenly we were being forced to exert ourselves. We didn't have the slow ox carts or any cannons with us, but nobody seemed to be in much of a hurry. The Mexicans had a number of spare horses, but they insisted that our officers walk. They might have made life easier on our wounded too, but the Mexicans paid them little mind.

"At least we're better off than those poor wretches at the Alamo," Dr. Barnard told me. It really wasn't much comfort.

My mutilated shoe, which had been shot up when I ran out to see Josh, quickly became a problem, and I was so parched I felt I would collapse. I lagged farther and farther behind, and that only made matters worse. The men in front stirred up choking clouds of dust. When I recognized the little trail that led to Rancho Espinosa, I was sorely tempted to try and escape.

"I know what you're thinking," Andrew whispered as he helped me trudge along. "I've considered it too. Just look at the lancers on both sides of us, though. You wouldn't get a hundred yards."

Pa came back to check on me once or twice too, but he had an obligation to the rest of the Mobile boys, and he never stayed long. Sam Sagler walked with Andrew and me for a time, as did his father.

"Josh wanted to stay," Sam reminded me. That didn't make either one of us feel a bit better, though. I couldn't imagine what sorrow Mrs. Sagler would feel when she learned that she had two dead sons. The Saglers were also worried that the Mexicans would shoot them no matter what was done to the rest of us. Since the Saglers were citizens of Mexico, they were now considered traitors. I tried to look at Hernando's enlistment in the cavalry in such a light, but I still felt a little betrayed. The Espinosas had befriended me. Now they were my enemies.

By the time we approached the old fort that afternoon, I was nearing exhaustion. We forded the river as before, but most of us ducked our heads and swallowed as much of the river as we could. We were soaked from head to toe as a result, and it was hard not to feel resentment when the Mexicans looted our baggage and refused to let us change into dry clothes. We still got nothing to eat, and I was ushered into the church and made to sit on the cold floor, shivering.

I might have remained there if it hadn't been for Dr. Barnard. He sent for me to help with the wounded, and the work kept me on my feet and active so that I warmed up. He lent me a shirt to wear, and I skinned out of my own clothes. I felt a little naked, but the shirt covered everything important. I looked an odd sight, though, especially when my hair dried. Pieces of it stuck out in some mighty peculiar directions, and it brought smiles to the faces of my wounded companions.

I wasn't given any hard work to do in our little makeshift hospital, which was also inside the church. Mostly I fetched water from the well or washed faces. The next morning, Dr. Barnard talked the Mexicans into making us some soup, and we fed those well enough to tolerate it a thickish mixture of bacon and beans. I had some myself, and it wasn't altogether bad.

We had the first cheering news that afternoon when a considerable number of prisoners were brought in from Refugio. We thought they had all been killed, and they were afraid that we had, likewise, been slaughtered. We had a fine reunion, and the Mexicans even let one fellow have his fiddle back so we could have a little music.

Another 80 men were also brought into our camp. They
had landed on the coast and were captured at Copano,
right as they stepped off their boat. These men were put to
heavy labor.

The rest of our wounded arrived in carts, and I helped
these suffering men onto blankets. We had wood enough
to make cots, but we weren't allowed. Later, when the
Mexicans brought their own wounded to the fort, they
insisted on them having beds of a sort. It was funny. The
wounded of both sides were in the church together, and all
they had to do was look around to see their enemy. I
counted 60 Mexicans inside the church, and there were
other groups outside. It seemed that our riflemen had
done good work.

I tried to hate the Mexicans for killing Josh, but the
ones I saw were just poor fellows doing their duty. Most
were drafted into the army and were hundreds of miles
from home. One wounded man introduced himself as
Juan Flores. He only knew a few words of English, and I
didn't know much Spanish. Still, we managed to babble
away with each other whenever I brought him soup or
changed his bandage. Juan could draw anything he saw,
and he did a fine sketch of my face for me. He loved
flowers too, and I managed to pluck a few wildflowers for
him when I was sent to the river to wash linen on
Thursday.

Since Easter was near, the more religious among the
men organized some services. The Mexicans had a priest
with them who visited the wounded and prayed with them.

I wasn't Catholic, but I had a lot of respect for that priest. He raised spirits in men who were clearly near death, and he had a soft-spoken manner about him. Padre José, the men called him, but he was actually an Irishman. He had been in Mexico 20 years, though, and his speech rarely betrayed his origins. It was Father Joe, as I called him, who introduced me to Alejandro Ruiz.

Alejandro couldn't have been much older than me, and though his shoulders were broader, he was a full three inches shorter. He was from Matamoras, the town the ill-fated Texians had planned to capture, and he'd joined the army to be with his older brother, a lieutenant in the lancers. Mexico had suffered a bad outbreak of cholera months earlier, and Alejandro's parents, younger brothers, and sister all had perished. As Father Joe told it, the boy had nowhere to go but to his brother, who had enlisted Alejandro as the personal orderly to his company commander.

Alejandro was supposed to stay well to the rear, but boys have a bad habit of nosing around the front lines. One of our cannons blasted the spot where Alejandro was doing his nosing about, and pieces of the iron ball had torn off his left arm and mangled most of the rest of him. The others couldn't bear looking at his crushed chest and stump of an arm, but I kind of looked forward to my time with him. His eyes were bright green, and he never failed to thank me for bathing or bandaging or feeding him. He seemed to be getting better, but he caught a fever Friday morning and died at dusk.

His brother Felipe was there at the end, holding Alejandro's remaining hand. I was there too, trying once again to hold back tears. When Alejandro's chest rose and fell and then was still, his brother gently closed Alejandro's eyes and kissed his forehead. He stepped to my side, and in quite excellent English thanked me for being his brother's friend.

"I'm not sure we were friends," I confessed. "It's my people who killed him."

"Yes, but we're not enemies now," he assured me. "You helped ease my brother's pain. I could do nothing to help. We are different people, but we are still people."

"Can I ask you something, lieutenant?" I said, nervously studying his eyes.

"Anything," he replied.

"When are we going to march to Copano? When will they start sending us to New Orleans?"

Sad as he was over the death of his brother, he appeared to grow even sadder to hear my question. He glanced off toward the door, and I thought he would leave. He didn't, though.

"For your kindness," he told me, pressing a silver peso into my hand.

"I can't accept money," I argued.

"Keep it," he urged. "You may have use for it."

"But what about the ship to New Orleans? When will we be leaving here?

"My friend, the only true freedom from the troubles of this life is the freedom that my brother has found," Felipe said, gripping my shoulders. "Perhaps when you go to the river, you may become lost."

I looked at him with confused eyes. He would say nothing more, though, and when another officer appeared, he ordered us to carry his brother outside. Father Joe took charge of the arrangements, and a feverish lancer was brought in to occupy Alejandro's space.

I hadn't been particularly concerned about my safety before, but now I had an uneasy feeling. That night, after bringing soup to the wounded, I slipped outside and approached the huddle of men kept penned in the center of the parade ground. A soldier stopped me, but I told him my father was there. "*Mi padre*," I said, pointing to where Pa was sitting with the rest of the Mobile soldiers.

The soldier blocked my path with his rifle, but I showed him Lieutenant Ruiz's silver coin. The man pocketed the peso and let me pass.

When I reached Pa, his whole face lit up. He pulled me down beside him and gave me a rare hug.

"Pa?" I asked.

"I suppose you're too old for such things, but I haven't seen you in a while. I worry about you."

"They keep me pretty busy in the hospital," I explained. "I don't think they like the *medicos* to come out here."

"*Medicos?*" Pa asked. "You're learning Spanish, are you? I never could get you to pay it any mind in Mobile."

"I wish I'd listened better, Pa. Wish I'd done a lot of things differently."

"Well, I have the same thoughts these days," he confessed.

"Still trust in signs?" I asked.

"Well, I don't have a lot of my old notions these days, son. Still, we've got a house, and if Sam Houston is able to muster an army and make a fight of it, we might still come out of this with a place of our own."

"Are we going to come out of this?" I asked. "I had an odd talk with a Mexican lieutenant a little while ago. I don't think he believes we're going anywhere."

"Lieutenants don't issue orders, Jefferson. He wouldn't know what's in store for us. Colonel Fannin's told us about the terms. We're to be returned to the United States on condition that we never again bear arms against Mexico."

"Then why bring those fellows up here from Copano?" I asked. "Why not send them—and maybe some of us— back to New Orleans on the boat that brought them? I don't like to think about it, but a lot of the Mexican cavalry's ridden off toward the Guadalupe River. The soldiers who are still here won't look me in the eye."

"They're country boys, most of them, Jefferson. They're shy as a rule, and they keep to themselves. You can't expect them to jabber away when they don't even know your language."

I might have agreed except that until recently they had talked all the time. I couldn't help fretting about it.

"You can't always be worrying about everything, son," Pa told me. "A man doesn't control his life. He just does his best to survive. Some day you'll have children of your own and you'll need to have this same sort of talk. When you were little, you probably thought I could make every ounce of pain in your life go away just by whistling up the right tune on a mouth organ, but it doesn't work that way."

"I know, Pa."

"I wish you and Madison had been able to stay boys a little longer, but it doesn't appear that's going to happen. I haven't told you as often as I should have how proud I am of you. Bringing the supplies all the way from Columbia! Rushing out to fetch those water jugs. Helping the doctors tend our wounded. Son, I don't believe even I could have expected more of you, and you know I expect a lot sometimes."

"Sometimes?" I asked. "Always."

"Well, I just want to tell you that tonight I'll sleep a little better knowing that you'll be there to look after your ma and the family if something should happen to me."

"What?"

"Nothing I know of, Jefferson," he said, calming me. "I just wanted to get the words said. It may be that they send us marching to the coast before long. They might keep you at the hospital, though. If we get separated, don't let it worry you. We'll find each other in the end."

"We did here in Goliad, didn't we?"

"Sure did," he agreed. "Now it's turned late, and you're certain to have work waiting. Get some rest, though. They may march us hard."

Talk of marching to the coast cheered me, and I tried

to cast away my gloomy thoughts. When Lieutenant Ruiz brought me Alejandro's shoes the next morning, he told me that I might have need of them soon.

"I think the river finished the others," I confessed. "I guess we're marching to the coast then soon?"

"Sunday," he told me. "You will be marching on Sunday."

"It's Palm Sunday too," I told him.

"A holy day," he said, nodding. "God be with you, my little friend."

"With you too," I added. "This year it's also my birthday. I'll be 14."

"Fourteen," he said, chewing on the words. "Too young to be a soldier. Maybe—" He started to say something but stopped. He glanced around, spotted two officers standing by the door, and frowned. "Wear the shoes," he whispered. "Get plenty of rest. You may have a hard journey to make."

"All the way to Copano. Is it a hard march?"

"This will be hard, yes," he observed. "Very hard."

# Chapter 8

## Palm Sunday

That night Colonel Fannin appeared with a German officer who was serving in the Mexican army. They had been down to Copano to employ a ship for transporting us home, and the colonel announced that arrangements had been finalized.

"Boys, some of you are going to have to be patient," he explained. "There won't be room for everybody. We'll start out with the ablest group. The rest will be taken off to do some work for the Mexicans. The wounded, once their health is restored, will go last."

The news we were waiting for had finally arrived. The fiddler started up his music, and a man with a flute joined in. There was a lot of singing and celebrating that night despite the fact that we were still on thin rations. I did get some cooked beef to go with my soup, though, and

Hernando Espinosa brought some tortillas, a gift from Carla.

"In honor of the holy days," he told me as he passed them into my hands.

I only ate one. The others I gave to Pa to share with the Mobile boys.

That night I had my first truly good sleep since arriving back in Goliad. I was more than relieved to know that Pa would soon be headed home. The Mobile and New Orleans boys were going first, Pa told me. The Mexicans, too, seemed more relaxed by the news. Many of those who had demonstrated friendship circulated among our men, giving them little gifts of food. I noticed a lot of officers visiting the hospital and inspecting the wounded—theirs and ours. Felipe Ruiz, who spoke better English than most, explained that we *medicos* would remain to care for the wounded. Oddly, though, he brought me a woven coat that had belonged to Alejandro. He then had me kneel and say a prayer with him for his brother's soul.

Morning found the fort astir with activity. A Mexican colonel named José de la Portilla was now in command, and he ordered that our men be formed into columns. It struck me odd that a large, heavily armed escort was waiting outside for the first group. I supposed they were afraid of trouble, for it was well known that the New Orleans and Mobile groups had wanted to fight on. The Mexicans believed that the ammunition wagon explosion had been no accident, and those of our men who had retained sidearms or even knives were searched. Any possible weapon was confiscated.

More troubling to me was the decision to take all our wounded out into the open air. The Mexicans wanted to use the church for their own sick and wounded, but many of our men were still suffering and didn't benefit from being jostled about.

A group of soldiers then arrived and forced us to one end of the church at bayonet point. "We're *medicos*," I insisted. Father Joe tried to intercede for us too, but they ignored him. Finally three Mexican officers appeared and ordered the soldiers outside.

"You will go with the others," a captain explained, pointing to the door.

"All but the doctors," a second one announced. He was staring at Andrew and me, along with several others who had been helping there.

Lieutenant Ruiz then said something to the others. When they left, he led Andrew and me into a side room. It was a small storeroom, filled with piles of baggage. He ushered us in there and motioned us to get down on our knees. "I will come for you later," he explained.

I was now totally confused, and Andrew was even paler than usual. A bit of sunburn he'd picked up during the battle had passed—and fair-haired as he was, the time in the church had made him about the whitest body I'd ever seen.

"Something's wrong," he told me. "Why should we hide?"

I couldn't help remembering the coat and the evasive way the lieutenant had acted when I talked of going home. The Mexicans were not bringing in wounded to replace the men who had been carried out. Before I had a chance to dwell on things, though, three Mexican soldiers appeared in the storeroom. They had bayonets attached to the end of their muskets, and they poked them into trunks and bundles, laughing. Our little hiding place wasn't big enough for both Andrew and me, so when they turned their bayonets toward us I panicked. Andrew started to rise, but I pushed him down. I wasn't sure what was happening, but I suspected something had gone terribly wrong.

"There's not room," he whispered.

I nodded my head and tried to crawl toward the trunks. A pair of hands grabbed me by my legs and pulled me out into the center of the storeroom. I couldn't understand all the words, but I think they said something about finding a rat. I got to my feet, and one of the soldiers forced me out of the church at bayonet point.

By then the last of the three columns of men was headed out the gate. I expected to be added to that bunch, but Lieutenant Ruiz motioned to my bandaged arm. The soldiers forced me to sit among the wounded.

"What's happening?" the men asked me.

"That priest gave me a rosary," one of them said. "He knows I'm Catholic."

In a matter of minutes, things became clear. Drummers had led the three columns out of the fort, but they now stopped their beating. We could hear nervous voices shouting orders in Spanish. Then muskets opened fire.

"No!" I shouted, jumping to my feet.

A bayonet persuaded me to sit down. Mexican sergeants then barked orders, and to my horror a party of soldiers approached our wounded. Some of them smiled, while others had tears in their eyes. They started at the far end and drove bayonets into the pitiful wretches lying helpless on the ground.

"Why?" I asked the guards nearest me. They didn't understand or else ignored me. I could hear Colonel Fannin arguing with someone, insisting he had been promised safe passage to New Orleans.

That was when Hernando arrived. His eyes were wild, and there were blood splatters on his boots. Carla was with him. They argued with the guards for a minute and then grabbed me by both arms.

"What—" I started to say.

"No English," Hernando scolded. "You are our cousin. Put on that coat."

"Understand?" Carla added.

I nodded my head, but I understood nothing. It was too hot to be wearing a coat, but it did conceal most of me. Satisfied, the two of them dragged me out toward the gate, hammering away at me in Spanish while the Mexican soldiers laughed. Once outside the fort, Carla led me to a waiting horse.

"I can't ride," I told her.

"It's a gentle horse," she assured me. "Take a deep

breath and let Hernando help you up. Say nothing. Do nothing. Just follow me."

Hernando boosted me up atop the horse, and Carla led the way down the road. The shooting was continuing, both inside and outside the fort. Screams tore through the air. We made our way northward for a time. Then I saw with my own eyes the first column of men—or what was left of it. The Mexican soldiers had shot better than 80 men there. Now they were stripping the bodies. The few who were trying to crawl away were stopped by bayonet thrusts. I spotted a slim figure with reddish hair, and I thought my heart would stop. Then I saw Pa.

Carla must have realized what was happening because she slapped my horse's rump. The animal galloped away, muffling the words I wanted to shout. It was all I could do to hang onto the racing horse's neck and stay mounted. After a quarter of a mile, the horse slowed and Carla reached me.

"My father," I said, pointing back toward the road.

"I didn't know," she said. "We would not have come this way."

"He's dead," I said, shuddering as the impact of it all struck me. "Dead! They've killed him."

"They killed all of them," she said, spitting at the ground. "On a holy day. Nothing good will come of this."

"Why?" I asked. "I thought—"

"Do you think it is a coincidence that General Urrea has gone?" she asked. "No, this is the order of El Presidente. It is what he always does to prisoners."

"And me?" I asked.

**87**

"You must come to my grandmother's rancho. You can have some of Hernando's clothes. Your hair is dark. No one will suspect you are not a cousin."

"I can't stay," I argued. "Not after what they did to Pa. I've got to get back to Columbia and help my family."

"No," she said, pausing long enough to point to a Mexican patrol a hundred yards away. "They will find you, Jefferson Byrd. They will kill you too."

"Probably," I admitted. "But I can't stay here."

"Because we are Mexicans?" she asked. "Because Mexicans killed your friend and your father?"

"No," I said, wiping my eyes. "Because I promised Pa that I would look after Ma if the worst happened. I'm little good as a soldier, and I can hardly ride a horse. I keep my promises, though, Carla."

She softened some then. Nodding somberly, she turned us toward the river. We splashed across and continued to Rancho Espinosa. I had little trouble with the horse that day. I was mostly numb from shock.

Magdalena Espinosa met us at the arched entry to her home and turned our horses over to stable hands. She then led me inside, where Miguel took charge of me. He took me down a hall to the room he shared with Pablo. Nobody said anything, but it appeared to me that they all knew what had happened. Apparently everyone knew but the prisoners.

I should have figured it out. Hadn't the lieutenant given me enough warnings? I should have noticed the eyes of the soldiers when they took our wounded outside.

Perhaps if I had known Spanish better, I might have understood what was being said. But in the end, I guess we believed we were going home because it was what we wanted to hear. No one would have considered that, after surrendering honorably, we could be taken out and shot like wild dogs!

I sat for a few moments on the edge of Miguel's bed. Then a sharp pain flooded my belly, and I doubled over. As he leaned beside me, a great terrible sob erupted from deep inside me, and I started crying. I wouldn't have believed it possible. Of all the times! I was safe now, wasn't I? All I could think about was how Pa must have felt when the shooting started. He wouldn't know I was safe. He would see the eyes of those Alabama youngsters he had persuaded to surrender and he would feel responsible for their shortened lives.

I thought about Mrs. Sagler. Her grief had doubled that morning. She now had no husband. Three sons were dead. How many other mothers would never even know what had happened to their sons? The Mexicans wouldn't go bragging about what they had done.

As my grief poured out of me, I realized that Miguel was talking. I had one of my hands around his wrist and was squeezing so tightly I was leaving marks.

"I'm sorry," I said, releasing him. "I didn't mean to hurt you."

"I know," he said, sitting beside me. "We are brothers, remember?"

"Carla said cousins," I explained.

"One is the same as the other," he said, trying to manage a grin. "I was told to give you clothes to wear. They're here, on the chest," he added, pointing to a pair of trousers, some drawers, and a clean shirt. "Your shoes will do. Grandmother will trim your hair, and she has some oil that will darken your skin. You will look like me, I think."

"I won't be staying," I insisted.

"No, I didn't think you would," he told me. "Your friend, Josh, was killed, *sí?*"

"*Sí,*" I replied. "My father too."

"Mine as well," he said, frowning, "for speaking in favor of the miners of Zacatecas. Hernando says they shot thousands of rebels there. I think that is why he joined the army, to show we are not all traitors."

"It won't help you, me being here."

"Ah, they would have to fight Grandmother to look for you," Miguel said, laughing. "Not even a general dares to fight such a formidable enemy."

I nodded my agreement and pulled off the woven coat. Miguel pointed again to the clothes and left me to undress. Setting aside my old clothes was hard. I felt as if I was turning my back on Pa, on the cause for which he had given his life. I deemed it ungrateful to put my rescuers at risk, though.

Miguel returned with something to eat. I didn't feel hungry, but I surprised myself by gobbling down every bite. I emptied a pitcher of water as well. Later, Carla led me back outside. She had built a small log fire behind the stables, but she wanted my permission before setting my clothes alight.

"It's best?" I asked.

She nodded, and I threw the rags into the flames. They weren't the only things to burn. Three tall plumes of smoke rose from the direction of Goliad. The Mexicans had chosen to burn the corpses of their victims. Only charred bones would remain.

That afternoon the sound of approaching horses drew our attention. I dashed inside the house and hid beneath Miguel's bed. It proved unnecessary, though. Hernando had come to the rancho with a surprise. Andrew Case— who would never pass for any Mexican's cousin—climbed off a speckled mare. When he stepped into Miguel's room, I couldn't conceal my joy.

Later Andrew told me, "They shot almost everyone— Major Ward and the men from Refugio. Only those fellows taken at Copano were spared. They got captured before they could get their weapons, so they were never in armed revolt. I don't think a one of them's sleeping very well."

"They killed Pa," I said, shuddering as I remembered his lifeless eyes.

"Don't be sure," Andrew said, gripping my wrists. "I thought you were dead too, but here you are. A lot of the boys got away. I don't think all of the Mexicans were hot to shoot down unarmed men."

"I saw Pa," I said, letting loose a long breath. "They killed him, all right."

"Well, Dr. Barnard's safe and most of the others in the

hospital. They would have killed me but for catching you."

"Well, I wasn't trying to get caught," I insisted.

"It was Lieutenant Ruiz who smuggled me out. Then I met this bugler fellow who offered me the use of a horse. I figured maybe that was your doing too."

"No. I think they would help anyone, these people."

The whole Espinosa family gathered for dinner that evening. I sat between Miguel and Pablo as an honored cousin. Andrew was on the opposite side of the table between Carla and Hernando. The two señoras were at opposite ends. Two empty chairs were there too, and I couldn't help thinking of their dead husbands or the fallen uncle.

We ate a fine dinner as befitted a holy Sunday. For that brief time there was no talk of war or death. There were prayers for the departed souls, but I didn't know if that was an ordinary part of the feast or not. After we had gorged ourselves on baked chicken and roasted beef and boiled potatoes and carrots, Hernando led me outside to look at the stars. It was cloudy, so we could only see a few.

"I guess this is as good a time as any to thank you for my life," I told him.

"Ah, that was Carla's doing," he told me.

"She never could have gained entry into the fort without you," I argued. "I don't think it was Carla at all."

"Jefferson, I am a Mexican soldier," he said, stiffening. "I follow the orders of my officers. But I also must follow the laws of God. What was done today, on this day of all

days, was not God's will. No Mexican will be proud of
killing unarmed men, even enemies of our republic. You
weren't the only one saved. Many young men were taken
in by families here and in Goliad. One woman alone may
have saved all the soldiers from Copano."

"Why me, though?" I asked. "Why did *you* save *me?*"

"Because one can be an enemy and still be a man. I
saw how you helped our wounded. I watched when you
prayed with the lieutenant for the soul of his brother. You
didn't know all the right words, but your heart told you
what to say."

"He was just a young boy."

"Older than you," Hernando said, taking out a small
pouch and handing it to me. "From Lieutenant Ruiz. He
said to tell you it was in celebration of your birthday and
your life."

I stared at my feet. I had completely forgotten the date.
March 27. I was 14 now.

"There is money here to help you on your journey," he
explained.

"You understand why I have to go?"

"Of course," he said, nodding somberly. "I have
brought your friend to help you. Tomorrow I, too, must
leave. My company rejoins General Urrea. Miguel says
that you are his brother, so we too must be related. I wish
you a safe journey home to your family. You've seen the
face of war. Don't come back to it."

"I can't promise that."

"I understand. When we next meet, it will be as

enemies again. I pray it will not be my task to end your
life."

"You saved it, Hernando. I suppose it's yours to take. I
just pray it's not my fate to take yours."

"I would be happier if you would not," he said,
grinning. We clasped hands and made our peace, at least
for that night.

"You should get some rest," Hernando advised. "It's a
long way to Rio Brazos. We have three armies in your
way."

"Won't be easy getting through," I observed. But then,
what *had* been easy of late? Absolutely nothing.

# Chapter 9

## Hunted

Andrew and I left a little after dawn the following morning. Carla offered us a pair of horses that had belonged to one of the murdered Texian officers.

"There's food in here to last awhile," she said when she led us to the animals. "Try to stay off the road. Keep away from the settlements. Santa Anna's main army is 40 miles north of here, but the cavalry is spread from the coast northward. They're the ones to watch out for."

"You wouldn't have a rifle you could loan us, would you?" Andrew asked.

"I brought you these horses so that, if you're caught, they cannot trace them to us," Carla explained. "Do you think I would offer you the gun that might kill my brother? It's an odd thing. I have always considered myself a Tejano, and this has been my home since I could walk.

My friends and neighbors say one must be either a
Mexican or an enemy. Tejanos died at the Alamo, and
many of them ride with Sam Houston."

"They're just afraid," I said, touching her hand. "You
can't blame them, not after all the killing. A rifle wouldn't
do much good against a company of cavalry anyway. We're
better off traveling light."

She smiled and Andrew dropped the matter. Once we
were out of sight of the rancho, he grumbled some. I
hushed him.

"They risked everything for a pair of strangers," I told
him. "I don't know that I would have had the courage to
walk into a fort and claim a boy awaiting execution as *my*
cousin. Who cares about a fool rifle? We've got our lives,
don't we?"

Andrew set a hard pace that morning, and at times it
was all I could manage to stay in the saddle. By noon I was
aching in a dozen places. I pleaded for a halt so we could
rest ourselves and the horses. I was also starving, and the
break gave us a chance to eat. Although Andrew was
leading the way, he didn't know the country, so I found
myself drawing a map in the dirt to show him the way to
Guadalupe Victoria.

"We can't travel on the road, but it's probably just as
well," I told him. "It wasn't much more than a cart path,
and there aren't any bridges. You have to find a ford or
swim across."

I could see how happy that made him.

Shortly after stopping, I heard a sound in the high

grass behind us. I turned and examined the ground carefully.

"Probably a rabbit," Andrew declared.

"Don't bet on it," I said, dropping to my knees and inching toward the sound. Something stirred again, and I could tell it was a lot bigger than a rabbit. Just as I was about to call out to Andrew, someone grabbed me from behind and jammed my face into the ground.

"I got him!" a voice called triumphantly.

"Well, good for you," Andrew cried. "You fool. Don't you recognize me?"

"It's Andy Case," my captor said, relaxing his grip on me. "What you doing out here with a Mexican?"

"I'm not Mexican," I said, squirming away from my tormentor. "I'm Jeff Byrd."

"His pa was a sergeant in the Mobile Grays," Andrew explained.

"Alabama boy?" a second stranger asked.

"Was for about a year," I explained as I rolled free. Standing above me was a lanky fellow with the ragged remains of a uniform. His left arm was wrapped in bandages from the wrist to the shoulder.

"I'm Noah Johnson," he explained as he helped me to my feet. "Once corporal of the New Orleans Grays. I knew your pa."

"Zeke Taylor," the other man said, offering his hand. "I guess you know they shot most of us."

"How did you get away?" Andrew asked.

"Hid at the bottom of the pile of bodies," Noah

explained. "Then when they weren't looking, we got away."

"Any others?" I asked, offering some of our food. Noah accepted a share, but Zeke shook his head.

"Caught two catfish awhile back," he said, tapping his belly. "Got enough."

"There are a few of us out here," Noah said, frowning, "enough so the cavalry's scouring the countryside. We found one of the Rovers a mile back with his throat cut. There was a fresh grave nearby. I suspect he gave an account of himself."

"Hard to do when you don't have a rifle," Andrew complained.

"Well, you've got less to lug that way too, youngster," Zeke insisted. "Know anything about this country? I've got no sense as to where we are."

"We're north of the road to Guadalupe Victoria," I explained. "Maybe half a mile. Josh Sagler and I came out from there with a wagon. We forded the river north of town, so we ought to be fine if we head due east."

"You got a compass?" Noah asked.

"Only the one in my head," I said, grinning as I remembered Josh's mental map. "You can roughly follow the sun."

"That'll work," Zeke agreed. "You boys mind sharing your mounts?"

"We can take turns riding," Andrew suggested. "That way we can keep the walkers fresh."

"Good notion," Noah agreed. He even suggested

Andrew and I start out riding. When I figured an hour was up, I suggested trading with the others.

"I've got no watch," Andrew argued. "Who's going to know how much time's passed?"

"They look close to done in," I told him. Zeke and Noah were falling behind, and I judged they had been on their feet since the shooting had stopped. Andrew reluctantly dismounted, and I did likewise. The others thanked us for our kindness and climbed atop our horses. Then they slapped the animals and rode off at a gallop.

"Now what?" Andrew said, glaring at me angrily.

"Maybe they'll come back," I suggested.

"Sure, they will," he said, gazing to the east. "Well, you weren't too keen on riding anyway. Lead the way."

I frowned and waved him along. Taking our horses was a mean trick, but I guess lying at the bottom of a pile of dead men will turn you a little crazy. As for casting us afoot, I figured we'd have an easier time forgetting and forgiving that than they would.

We must have journeyed half of the 20-or-so miles to the Guadalupe River that day. On three occasions we spied Mexican cavalry. Each time we hid in the tall grass and let them pass.

"There are some advantages to being afoot," I told Andrew.

"Not many," he said, wincing as we resumed our walking. That night I tended his blistered feet. We shared what was left of my food. Andrew had left his tied to his saddle. I could only hope that we would get close enough to the settlements before long to find food and help.

The help we eventually found was named Patrick Lynch. He was hiding in the reeds along the Guadalupe when we got there. Just 12 years old, with his clothes torn to shreds by briers, he raced out and greeted us like a long-lost brother.

"Who are you?" I asked, prying his arms from my waist.

That's when he broke down crying. It turned out that Patrick was one of the settlers who came out from Ireland. His pa had joined the army, and the rest of his family was in a wagon headed for safer ground east of the Brazos. He had agreed to stay and feed the livestock.

"So what are you doing here?" Andrew asked.

"The Mexicans came," he explained. "Took everything they could carry. Shot everything else. They were in a mean mood. I showed 'em my crucifix and spoke to them in Spanish, but one took a shot at me anyway. Nicked my ear," he added, showing us. "I took off running and didn't stop till I got to the river."

"Isn't Houston here?" I asked.

"He's somewhere, but he's sure not here. Mostly Mexican cavalry all along the river, hunting for some of our boys who ran away from Goliad. That'd be you?"

"Guess so," I said.

Patrick stepped back and glared at us.

"Cowards," he growled. "Expected you fellows with Fannin to stand your ground and keep the enemy away from our homes. Instead you fall apart and run off!"

That was when it dawned on me that no one knew
what had really happened. As I told Patrick about the
hopeless battle—how, despite our poor position, we held
off every enemy charge—he softened his resentment. I let
Andrew tell about the murder of the prisoners.

"We'll all die, won't we?" he asked.

"Haven't bagged us yet," I pointed out. "Know where
there's some food to be had?"

"I've got a fishing pole," he replied.

With Andrew or me standing guard, Patrick managed
to snag three fat channel catfish from the Guadalupe. We
cooked them over a small fire built with seasoned wood so
as to keep down the smoke. There were farmhouses
burning all around us, and Patrick said the cavalry wasn't
likely to pay much attention to a wisp or two from the
river. I wanted—in fact needed—to believe it.

We'd hardly finished our supper, though, when a 10-
man cavalry patrol appeared. "That's done it," Andrew
complained as we scampered for cover in the higher grass
on a nearby hill.

I halfway believed it, but Patrick knew that stretch of
river. He guided us to a fallen oak tree, and we burrowed
into the soft ground nearby. It provided a good hiding
place, and the cavalrymen quickly tired of looking for us.
Once they left, Andrew and I decided that the sooner we
were across the river, the better it would be for us. Little
Patrick insisted on staying.

"Ma'll expect me to be hereabouts," he explained.
"Once the cavalry's on the far side of the Guadalupe, I'll

be safe enough. I can always hide under the tree again."

I gave him a pat on the back and left him my Mexican coat. I had tired of dragging it along. Besides, being with Andrew, there wasn't much point in trying to disguise myself as a Tejano.

"Thanks," he said as we turned to leave. "God watch over you."

"That's a welcome thought," I said, "but you watch out for Mexicans. They may nick more than your ear next time."

Andrew and I continued our flight eastward, but it grew more dangerous each day. We were constantly coming across whole companies of Mexican soldiers, looting the scattered settlements left by their terrified residents. Once, we walked into a house that had the dinner plates set out on the table. The coals had burned to ashes in the fireplace, but a pot of beef stew sat there where the cook had left it about a day and a half before. The stew was burned in places, and it was cold. Even so, we ate every bite of it.

The following morning we had our closest call. Three Mexican lancers came up on us out of a thick mist. We were all surprised, but they were quicker to act. One charged Andrew, and he had to scramble between two oaks to avoid being run through. The two that came at me did it proper. One stayed on each side, blocking any path of escape. They carried pistols, but they preferred using their iron-tipped lances. They edged their way closer, and I glanced around nervously, hoping to find some sort of cover. Then it came to me. The street in Charleston.

The ground was full of rocks, so I picked one up. Shouting furiously, I hurled it at the man on my left. He moved aside and allowed it to sail on harmlessly. That's when I turned and threw my second rock at his companion. We were only seven or eight feet apart, and I struck him squarely on the forehead. The man just fell back and rolled off his horse in a daze. The other lancer turned toward me but he couldn't steady his horse. I tossed my third rock at the animal's rump, and it galloped off, taking the frustrated cavalryman along.

I never even saw where the third lancer went, but Andrew appeared and waved me into a thick stand of thorny locust trees. We stayed there until the sounds of horses' hooves were farther and farther away. Then we made our way northward, away from the shouts and curses behind us.

The day we reached the Colorado River, I realized we had strayed too far from the road. I recognized nothing about that country. There were scarcely any settlers or even burned cabins where we made our crossing. We caught sight of fresh horse tracks, but there were never more than a few riders.

"What'll we do if we never catch up to the army?" Andrew asked.

"Which army?" I asked. "I'm not sure if there's even a Texian army left. Four or five thousand Mexican soldiers like the ones at Coleto Creek are too many for everyone in Texas to fight."

"No, they aren't," Andrew argued. "If we had stood our ground and fought it out along the creek or at Fort Defiance, we would have crippled that army. We shot it up some as it was. Even when we were without water, they had to lie in order to get us to surrender."

"We wouldn't have lasted another day, Andrew," I said, sighing. "All they had to do was wait us out."

He never did agree with me, and on we journeyed. On April 4, the evening before Easter Sunday, we finally stumbled onto some of Houston's scouts. There were just four of them, but seedier men you never saw in your whole life. They were dressed in buckskin boots, broad-brimmed beaver hats, and oversized shirts that hung down past their waists. Their leader, a quiet fellow named Smith, welcomed us to his camp. When he learned we'd been with Fannin, he had two of his companions take us to the general himself.

Houston's army, such as it was, was a hard day's ride farther east on the Brazos. Sitting atop one of Smith's spare ponies, I was jostled and bounced across the roughest trail I'd ever traveled. I was sure no Mexican army would find us there. They weren't stupid enough to travel the route.

We arrived long after dark. I was scratched from my head to my toes, and two considerable gashes in my left side were bleeding. Andrew was no better. In fact, his pale skin made him appear even more battered. A doctor took charge of us for a bit, but a little soap and water undid most of the damage. Once we were on our feet, General Houston arrived.

Houston was a tall, broad-shouldered man, but just then he didn't make much of an impression. His shirt hung outside his britches, and I suspected we might have interrupted his sleep.

"What news do you bring us of Fannin?" he began.

"Dead, sir," I answered. "Most of the command surrendered. The men at Refugio too. Last Sunday they marched most of the fellows out and shot 'em. My pa was with 'em."

"And how is it you survived?" Houston asked, studying us.

"We were lucky," I explained. "An officer hid us in the hospital, and some local people took us in for a time. We would have done better, but two men took our horses."

"Maybe not," the general said, showing us a provision bag. It was the one that Carla had given Andrew.

"They're here?" Andrew asked.

"We found the horses and the men," Houston said. "The horses went down first. The men were a time dying. They ran across part of General Sesma's column—the same men who killed Colonel Travis at San Antonio. Our boys killed a lot of them there, and the ones who survived turned ugly. Your friends found that out."

"They weren't friends," Andrew fumed. "Not after they stole our horses."

"You two might well be dead if you'd stayed mounted, son. We've had a handful of Fannin's men get through, but all of 'em's come on foot. I'll see to it that you youngsters get food and some new clothes. Do you have family hereabouts?"

"Only family I had died at the Alamo," Andrew announced. "I'm staying on to fight."

"You?" Houston asked, turning to me.

"My ma's in Columbia," I explained. "I'd best get down there and see that she's safe."

"That would surely be best," the general agreed. "I'm sending a party down there in the morning to secure the river crossings. They would probably enjoy your company."

"I wouldn't mind company myself," I replied.

"Get some rest, boys. I want to talk to you a little longer about what you've seen on the way here. Now it's best we all get some sleep, though."

# Chapter 10

## A Fork in the Road

The next morning I was up early. General Houston had ordered a party of horsemen to check the river crossings to the south. There were rumors that Santa Anna had left General Sesma to tie down the main force of Texians while he took his part of the army around to the south. We made the trip easily enough along the eastern bank of the river, but we spied Mexican scouts on the far bank. That made me quite anxious because that was the side of the river where our house stood.

By late afternoon we were across the river from Columbia itself. The town seemed quiet enough. Smoke rose from chimneys, but there wasn't a soul in sight. The scouts were dismayed that no one was watching the crossings. They sent two men back to inform Houston. The others decided among themselves who was going to watch which ford.

"My house isn't far," I told them. By that time I had gotten used to riding a horse, and I wasn't afraid of going ahead on my own. My rump ached from pounding against the saddle, but it was better than wearing out the soles of Alejandro's shoes.

"Best we send a man with you," declared the leader, Corporal Hunt.

"I wouldn't want to leave you short-handed," I insisted. "Besides, I'll probably have to swim across. No use in somebody else getting soaked."

"You watch yourself, hear?" the corporal shouted. "And come along back here if you don't find anybody."

I started to ask what he meant but decided against it. Why wouldn't Ma be at home? The Mexicans hadn't come that deep into our country yet. We hadn't seen enemy scouts for hours, and *somebody* was home in town.

I made my way along the bank, rehearsing how I would tell Ma about Pa. I'd never had anything so difficult to do in my whole life. There was Mrs. Sagler too. At least Pa had given me a letter. I would have to use my own words to explain about Josh and the others.

I saw Moses' sawmill first. Then a bit beyond there I spotted the big Sagler house atop its hill. I tied my horse to a small willow tree and skinned out of my clothes. Bundling them up and holding them over my head to keep them dry, I waded into the shallows. The river was deep, though, and I didn't manage to keep anything dry. I found a few trees out of clear sight of everywhere and set my wet clothes up in branches. Then I waited for them and me to dry.

Fortunately the sun was out, and that helped chase the worst of the chill from my bones. Pa had told me once that the best thing to do was to rub the wetness out of a body, so I did what I could to rub the damp wrinkles out of me. There were parts that were just plain unreachable, though. My hair was like a mop despite its recent cutting. I took a look at my reflection in the water and was stunned. My ribs were nearly sticking out of my skin, and I doubted I weighed 100 pounds. In Mobile a year before, I had been closer to 120 on the grain scales. And I'd added several inches of bone since then!

When I could think of nothing else to do, I began putting on my soggy clothes. Then I continued on foot to the house. To my surprise the door was open. The wind swung it to and fro, and I felt an icy chill run down my spine.

"Ma?" I called. "Maddy?"

I dashed up the porch steps and raced on inside, but the place was deserted. The trunks we had brought out from Mobile were gone. The cabinets Moses had crafted were empty. There wasn't a soul in sight. It was the same thing at the Sagler place, except most of the furniture remained. There was a note addressed to Josh, though. "Headed for Harrisburg," it read. That was all.

I went to the little cabin Moses used, but there were no signs of life there either. Disappointed, I returned to the river and started back across. I kept my clothes on this time, so I arrived a soggy wretch. I didn't bother drying myself this time. Instead, I rode back to the scouts and told them what I had seen.

"It's the same upriver," the corporal told me. "Panic. They're calling it the 'runaway scrape'! I've seen places where folks left their half-eaten breakfast on the table. At San Felipe, Stephen Austin's town, the whole population headed out. Pitiful folks, most of them. Even worse at Gonzales. Most of the men there had ridden down to help Travis, so it was mostly widows and orphans heading east."

Part of me ached to hear the story. Another part was boiling mad. "What would you do, Corporal, if the Mexicans chased your family out of their house?" I asked. "If they murdered your pa? If they did their best to stick you with lances and shot a musket ball through your arm?"

"I'd find me a rifle," he answered.

"Know where there's one to spare?"

"No, but I suspect the general can find you one. Welcome to the army, Jeff."

I had to wait for that rifle, though. I spent my first week in the Texian army helping the doctors treat sick men. The army was filling up with young men, and a lot of them suffered from mumps and measles. Because I'd had both of them while growing up in Charleston, the doctors felt safe putting the feverish young men in my care. There wasn't much more to do than what I'd done at Goliad. In truth, there was some comfort to the work. The busier I was, the less time I had to think about Ma and my brothers and sister. I wrote a letter to them and sent it with a courier to Harrisburg. I got no reply. They had seemingly vanished.

Our little army was about worn down to a nub, but things slowly began to improve. We were camped at the plantation of a man named Groce. Both wealthy and generous, he provided us with good food and clean clothes. His shops repaired our wagons, and gunsmiths repaired or rebuilt our damaged weapons. But perhaps most important, the army enjoyed a good, long rest. The weak and sick men recovered their health, and spirits soared. There were some quarrelsome elements in General Houston's army, but for a short while everyone seemed to be of one mind.

The army used its time in camp to train. Most of the men, even the youngest ones, knew how to shoot. They were brave to a fault. But few knew what it was like to stand in line and take on a determined enemy. I knew all too well how disciplined and determined the Mexicans could be.

On April 11 we got another morale boost. The citizens of Cincinnati, Ohio, sent us two small cannons. Nicknamed the "Twin Sisters," they were mounted on good carriages and easily maneuvered. Watching the men drill, I couldn't help feeling a new sense of confidence. I think the rest of the younger men felt it too. Now that we had a real army, though, it needed to do some fighting.

The following day, we broke camp and headed east again. Rumors abounded that Santa Anna was burning towns along the Brazos and sending his cavalry after innocent women and children. We saw for ourselves El Presidente's handiwork that week when we reached

Harrisburg. The Mexicans had burned the town, and a small army of citizens came to our camps to describe the looting that had gone on before the fires started.

Again I asked about my family, but there were so many people on the roads that no one remembered names. We set up a hospital there, and one of the surgeons, Dr. Keller, urged me to stay. I had passed enough time tending the sick, though. I went to find a rifle. With over two hundred men sick in a makeshift hospital, there were lots of unneeded weapons at hand.

"I guess you've come to a fork in the road," Andrew told me when he saw me examining the spare firearms. "Time to make our stand, huh?"

"We've done this before," I said as he handed me a good Kentucky rifle. "It's different this time, though. General Houston seems like the sort of man who knows his business."

"Just another officer who can't make up his mind," Andrew muttered. "You figure we're really going to fight this time?"

I believed so. Santa Anna was nearby with one wing of the Mexican army. There wasn't much of anywhere in Texas left for us to go. Some believed that Houston planned to lure the Mexicans to the border and draw the United States into the war. I can't speak for what the general was thinking, but the army wasn't going much farther. Our families were suffering. Most people had already lost their homes. It was time to plant crops and make new beginnings. We had to deal with the Mexicans once and for all.

So I guess we all had reached that fork in the road. General Houston must have figured it that way because he formed the army into a hollow square and spoke to us about his plans. He said we would soon face the enemy. Although some of us might be killed, he told us to think about the soldiers who had died at the Alamo.

"Remember the Alamo!" the men shouted.

He spoke of Goliad, and the men shouted, "Remember Goliad!"

I needed no speech to tell me to do that. Every night when I closed my eyes, I saw Pa's bloody body lying in the road, and I knew that Andrew was thinking of his brother Ben. There were others too, with friends or relatives among the slain heroes. Moreover, we knew that the man who had ordered the assault against the Alamo—the one who had ordered helpless prisoners shot—would soon face our rifles.

We made our way with renewed purpose down the narrow road that led from Harrisburg to the coast. Most of us were strangers to this part of the country, but I had a good feeling about the place. It was marshy, which meant that the Mexican cavalry would have a hard time of it. We stopped across from a body of water called Buffalo Bayou. The scouts swam their horses across, and some of the army, including General Houston, crossed on rafts.

The rest of us had to wait for a leaky steamboat to carry us over. I wasn't sure afterward whether we wouldn't have been better off swimming too. We formed our lines along an eerie line of trees that had Spanish moss hanging from their branches.

I had joined Andrew's company by that time. Most of the others were volunteers from Alabama and Georgia, so I felt at home. Once we got settled, Andrew taught me how to load, aim, and fire my rifle. It had a fair kick, and the two times that I actually fired the weapon left painful bruises. Still, I came close enough to the branch I was aiming at to feel confident that I wouldn't embarrass myself when the Mexicans arrived.

It was ground well chosen for our purpose. The San Jacinto River formed one edge, and the lip of Galveston Bay formed another. With the bayou to our backs, we had no choice but to advance on the ground in front of us. We had less than 1,000 men, but on that narrow strip of ground we had enough. There was no way 10,000 Mexicans could outnumber us on the front line. Moreover, most of our army lurked in the trees, so when Santa Anna sent a party of skirmishers forward, all he could see were our little cannons and a thin line of supporting infantry.

I don't think Santa Anna was all that serious about fighting that day. It was overcast, and there was a cold wind blowing off the water. If it started raining, we would have a tough time of it firing our rifles. The Mexicans at Goliad had carried heavy British-made muskets that often misfired. Of course, rain wouldn't help the cavalry either.

The Mexicans advanced slowly, displaying caution. Their buglers sounded an odd call—which, one of the Georgians explained, meant "no quarter." Well, what with word of the murder of our prisoners going around, I don't think anybody was surprised about that.

"It won't be us asking quarter anyway," Andrew whispered. "They'll be the ones begging for mercy."

I hoped he was right. The fighting was mostly foolishness that day, though. From about 50 yards away, the Mexicans exchanged shots with our cannons. Then Santa Anna himself appeared, riding a tall bay horse and wearing what looked like 20 shiny medals. I wished I had been close enough to get off a shot, but General Houston restrained the bulk of the army. There was some hot shooting for a time. General Houston had his horse's reins clipped, and Colonel Jim Neill, commanding the artillery, was hurt. A few Mexicans were also shot, but it was difficult to see if anybody was killed.

After the Mexican skirmishers retreated, they sent out a few horsemen to watch us. When they shouted curses at us, a few of our own horsemen charged them. These men, in turn, were driven back by the Mexicans. It seemed odd—so many men drawn up across from each other while only a few skirmished with each other. That's exactly what happened, though.

I really expected a full-blown battle, but General Houston waited. He seemed to be looking for an opening. We kept alert, and the Mexicans stood in their battle formations until sundown. That night I ate dried beef beside Andrew and wondered if the big battle everyone expected the next morning would come about. I halfway hoped it wouldn't. It was one thing to fire a rifle at a pecan tree. Shooting a person was something else.

I had a hard time getting to sleep. Each time I closed
my eyes, I found myself back at Coleto Creek, staring into
Josh's lifeless eyes. I awoke screaming twice. Finally I
walked off to the shore of the bayou and tried to find
some peace.

"Nervous, son?" a deep voice called. I turned and
found myself face-to-face with General Houston for the
second time that month. "Memories?" he asked.

"A few," I confessed.

"The night before a battle's always a difficult time," he
told me. "I don't sleep well myself. Come daybreak I'm
always sorry I didn't sleep, though. A rested soldier fares
better."

"I lost my pa at Goliad," I explained. "My best friend
too. Whenever I try to get some rest, I see one or the
other."

"Do you see those fires out there?" the general asked,
pointing to the Mexican camps. "Tomorrow we'll be
exchanging volleys with them. They're probably sleeping
soundly. Now, who's going to shoot straight?"

I caught sight of a grin spreading across his face, and I
matched it.

"You'll do all right, son," he said, patting my back.
"You know what's at stake. A man doesn't often get a
chance to right a wrong like the one that Texas has
suffered."

"No, sir," I agreed.

"Now get some rest."

"Yes, sir, " I said, heading back toward the trees.

# Chapter 11

## Victory or Death

Despite the general's urging, I got little sleep and even less peace that night. Memories of the fighting at Goliad streamed through my memory, and when a drum roused the army before dawn that next morning I fought off a terrible weariness. Worse, there was a harsh chill in the air, and I found myself shivering from more than fear.

"Come on, Jeff," Andrew said, shaking my shoulders. "We're forming our lines."

I tried to wriggle free, but his grip was like iron.

"Now!" he shouted.

I rolled out of the single blanket that the quartermasters had provided me, and the cold stung me like a thousand angry hornets.

"I know," Andrew said, trying to rub some warmth into me. "Wrap your blanket around you and come on.

Maybe we can get some breakfast."

"I thought we were forming battle lines," I complained.

"We will, but we have to eat something."

I wanted to ask, Since when? But everyone was rushing around to some purpose or another, and I didn't see any point in grumbling. A lot of the men were dressed in little more than rags, and Andrew had observed that if it weren't for the mud that caked the cloth, half the army would march out naked. The cold only made matters worse. I'd learned to expect sudden changes in the weather, but this was new.

"It's a blue norther'," an old man named Nelson explained. "It don't last, but it's a powerful vexation when it hits you."

"Especially when you're out in the open," I said, sipping a steaming cup of hot coffee that Andrew had passed to me.

"Before the day's out, the weather's apt to be the least of our troubles," Nelson went on to say. "Santa Anna's got us outnumbered as things are, and rumor has it there are more Mexicans marching this way. Hope we hit 'em before those other fellows arrive."

I figured the odds were already against us. The only thing we had going for us was that I never saw an army so mad. Old Grandpa Nelson had lost a son and two grandchildren at the Alamo. He no sooner finished gulping his coffee and cornbread than he started sharpening a big bowie knife.

"I aim to cut the heart out of the first Mexican I see," he declared.

"We're a bloodthirsty bunch, aren't we?" Andrew asked. He, too, had a hungry look in his eyes, and I knew it had nothing to do with the scant breakfast we'd eaten. He was thinking of his brother and our friends killed at Goliad.

Try as I could, I couldn't muster the same kind of hate. Nobody had lost more than I had, but men like those very Mexicans, together with the Espinosas, had saved my life. I had watched their ordered ranks at Coleto Creek, and I didn't see how we could break their line with a lot of shouting and cursing. They had seemed plenty calm the day before.

I thought maybe the plan was for us to march out in the morning fog and surprise Santa Anna's army, but General Houston slept until nearly eight o'clock. By then the mist had lifted, and the Mexicans had a line of infantry formed behind their earthen barricade. Shortly, a company of cavalrymen rode out on their left. They kept their distance, though.

We got our first reinforcements that morning. When I heard, I thought that maybe now our chances were better. But it turned out that the only ones who had come were nine youngsters who had rowed across the neck of Galveston Bay. You could tell they were newcomers because their clothes had no tears and the two old enough to grow whiskers were clean-shaven. They stared at us as if we had grown horns.

We must have made a comical sight: Our 800 soldiers
huddled around a couple dozen campfires. Nobody had
bathed since leaving Groce's place, and there were men
with heavy beards and hair down past their shoulders.
They came from everywhere too, and you could hear a
dozen languages spoken that morning. Most of the
Germans and Frenchmen also spoke passable English, and
some were veterans of European wars. Juan Seguin's
Tejanos were the fiercest. Some of them had been at the
Alamo until dispatched as scouts, and all of them had lost
friends and relatives there. Those fellows were looking for
blood, and I wouldn't have wanted to be in their way.

Our young reinforcements brought us news that Santa
Anna's brother-in-law, General Cos, was nearby with 500
veterans.

"Best attack before those fellows get here," Grandpa
Nelson said.

Although we had formed our lines, we didn't move a
step closer to the enemy. When the scouts rode in with a
message for the general, we all knew Cos had arrived. The
Mexicans were cheering, and there was dust coming from
the road to the west. The Mexicans soon increased their
cavalry force on our left. Now there were better than 500
mounted lancers there, threatening to charge our thin line.
Rumor had it that Santa Anna had another thousand or so
infantry formed behind the barricade and Cos's men
waiting in reserve.

Outnumbered as much as three to one, with only
water behind and to our sides, I didn't think our chances

were too great. Now that the sun was up, we weren't going to surprise anybody. If the general meant to wait for the Mexicans to attack, he'd done nothing to prepare us. Even at Coleto Creek, we'd dug trenches to shield us from musket and artillery fire.

The only thing we did that morning was send some of the scouts around the Mexicans' flank. I didn't learn until later that it was to burn a bridge. Doing so cut off any possibility of reinforcement or retreat. When the scouts returned, I already knew that they had burned the bridge, for smoke had been curling skyward in the rear of the Mexican cavalry. Around noon we were told to break ranks and get something to eat. The general called over all the officers, and they had a talk.

"Bet we're going to retreat again," Andrew grumbled, as he chewed a stick of dried meat.

"Where to?" I asked. "All the bridges are down now, and the steamboat's gone. We don't have any choice but to fight."

"Sure, but when?" Andrew asked.

Most of the army must have been asking the same question. As for the Mexicans, they withdrew their cavalry behind the barricade and relaxed their guard. I guess they gave up on our attack too.

I don't know what General Houston talked about with his colonels, but they were at it better than two hours. Sitting around our fires, we grew even more anxious than before.

"Nervous?" a sergeant named Ken Henderson asked me.

"A bit," I confessed.

"Don't be," he said, sitting beside me a moment. "I heard you lost your pa at Goliad. We'll give you your chance to square things before long."

"Why didn't we hit 'em early, before they got ready?" I asked.

"Damp air and powder don't mix," he told me. "You wouldn't want to make it a close-in fight, not with Mexican bayonets."

That made sense. I just couldn't understand why General Houston left us standing in line all that time if he meant to wait a day to make his attack.

I got my answer that same hour. Our officers hurried back to their commands, and the drummer, a big black man, beat the call to arms. Andrew dragged me along to where our little band was joining up with the rest of Company D of Colonel Ned Burleson's First Texas Regiment. We occupied the center, staring directly at the Mexican barricade. In places we were two men deep, but we weren't any deeper anywhere. The line was mighty thin, if you asked me. I was glad to see that the Mexicans weren't sending their cavalry back out. They could have done us some real damage.

Strangely, despite the noise of barked orders and the drum, now joined by three fifers, the Mexicans made no effort to confront us. Their camp was deathly quiet, as if the whole bunch of them had slipped away.

"You remember how quiet it got at Goliad in the afternoon," Andrew reminded me as we loaded our rifles. "Maybe they're having their siesta."

"They did that after eating," I argued. "What would they need to rest in the late afternoon for?"

Even if they were resting, I couldn't see why they wouldn't have a substantial guard watching us. We didn't even see sentries. They had no pickets out in front of their barricade. I couldn't help worrying that it was all some sort of devilish trap. They wanted us to march in close. Then they would let loose with their muskets and attack.

Our army didn't seem worried. Why would they be? They hadn't seen what General Urrea had done to Colonel Fannin. They only had their anger to guide their movements. That and whiskey. Grandpa Nelson was passing a bottle among the men. Several took more than a sip.

General Houston now made his way among the men, chatting and cheering them. I looked up and down our line and tried to muster my own courage. Our cavalry was on the far right, but there weren't a hundred of them altogether. To the left was Colonel Sidney Sherman's Second Texas Regiment. They were still partly concealed by trees. I figured that if things went well, they would skirt the barricade and hit the Mexicans on their flank. Besides us, the Twin Sisters supported the center of the line. Colonel Henry Millard had his two companies of regulars there too. Most of them were veterans of the U.S. Army and a few were on furlough from their regular duties with garrisons in Louisiana.

At Goliad, Colonel Fannin had had three or four brave flags flying. One had a white star and the inscription

*Independence* stitched on it. The only flag we carried that afternoon had a naked lady on it and the words *Victory or Death*—Colonel Travis's last message from the Alamo. It was enough to make a boy of 14 blush, and when the musicians took up a bawdy Irish song, I hoped Ma wouldn't learn about it. A powerful lot of cursing was going on that morning too.

"What would your ma say if she heard you talk like that?" I asked a little fellow named George East who wasn't any older than 13.

"It'd be a good deal worse if she knew I was here," he said, grinning at me.

General Houston, for all his delaying, now seemed intent on making an attack. He rode ahead of us on a tall white horse and shouted, "Forward!" And so we started across that field toward the Mexican barricade. I tried to concentrate on the ground just ahead of my feet and keep from bumping into the men around me. Andrew and I started behind the first line, but before we had gotten halfway, we were in front with everybody else. Colonel Sherman's men moved farther to the left, and we had more ground to occupy.

Maintaining a straight line on that soggy ground was hard. The artillerymen had a particularly difficult assignment. They had to drag the cannons along with rawhide ropes, and we halted every little bit to let them catch up. If the cannons could tear a gap in the barricade, we could maybe force a break in the Mexican line.

We marched slowly, with care, toward the enemy.

When we got to within 200 yards of the barricade,
General Houston ordered a halt. The Twin Sisters were
loaded, and they opened the fight with blasts of broken
horseshoes. The wicked chunks of iron blasted the
barricade, but the volley of musketry we expected to
answer never came. There was a shout or two, but no sign
of a Mexican line.

I'm not sure anyone gave the order to charge. A few
men here and there just started running, and the rest
followed. Grandpa Nelson drew out his knife and waved
us on. I took a deep breath and followed Andrew.

Shots rang out here and there, but I didn't see anybody
hit on either side. Seguin's men shouted all sorts of threats
in Spanish and finished with a bloodcurdling, "*Recuerden
el Alamo!*"

"Remember the Alamo!" others yelled.

"Remember Goliad!" I screamed.

"All for Texas!" Sergeant Henderson shouted.
"Forward, boys!"

Then a handful of Mexicans appeared at the top of the
barricade. Two were still loading their muskets. A tall man
wearing badges of rank appeared to be trying to get the
Mexicans' big 12-pounder cannon loaded. Andrew paused
and shot one of the Mexicans from the barricade. I turned
my rifle on a thin-faced man with an ugly scar on his
cheek. He aimed his musket at me, but I fired a second
before he could cock his weapon. My ball struck him in
the hip and knocked him down.

No one else bothered reloading, so I followed Andrew

toward the barricade. In a flash we were up and over it. To our surprise, there was no Mexican line waiting for us. Their camp was in chaos. Half-dressed men raced around screaming. Colonel Sherman's men were driving a third of the enemy from their tents. Their big muskets lay neatly stacked and beyond their reach.

I took a moment to reload my rifle. I had no big knife or any other weapon. Despite the chaos, I knew there were still plenty of armed Mexicans around. I walked over to the barricade to look for the thin-faced soldier, but he was gone. I hadn't hurt him very badly, I decided.

To my right, a line of Mexican infantry was forming. They fired a volley, and I dove to the ground unhurt. Others were less lucky. General Houston and another horseman went down. The general's horse was shot to pieces, but the general wasn't wounded. He soon found another mount and went on fighting. Later they shot him in the ankle, but he continued to direct at least some of the army.

Mostly, though, the battle turned into a bunch of sharp fights between a few men here and there. Nobody was really in charge. There were too many Texians with too much anger, and the Mexicans who weren't able to get organized perished in small clumps of three or four. Grandpa Nelson, true to his word, cut and slashed anybody he found. Andrew and I followed Sergeant Henderson around behind the Mexican cannon and fired on the men manning the gun. I don't know whether I actually hit anybody. I fired three shots there, and men fell, but there were a lot of people shooting at the cannon. The line that was holding back our cavalry broke apart next, and when our horsemen entered the Mexican camp the battle was as good as over. A tall general stood defiantly by the 12-pounder, and some of our officers ordered a cease-fire. I held my fire, but many didn't. This brave man—who I later learned was General Castrillon— was hit by at least five balls and fell dead where he stood.

The fighting was all but over, but the killing was only beginning. Sherman's men were chasing hundreds of enemy soldiers toward a lake, and a number of Mexicans were trying to escape westward down the road. We'd burned the bridge there, though. Most of the men who went that way were cut off by our cavalry and either killed or captured.

Andrew and I stuck with Sergeant Henderson. We didn't bother reloading. We used our rifles like clubs and subdued the few Mexicans with any fight left in them. Most threw up their arms and pleaded for their lives.

"No Alamo!" they would cry. "No Goliad."

I knew well enough that these weren't General Urrea's men, but a lot of those soldiers had watches or boots that had belonged to some of the men killed at the Alamo. Any poor fool with such souvenirs met with terrible vengeance.

We were fighting our way toward the cannon when three uniformed Mexicans appeared in front of us, muskets in hand. Staring into their wild eyes and looking at their sharp bayonets, I thought we were done for. A band of Kentuckians saw us, though, and they let loose a volley that tore those Mexicans to pieces.

"Best reload, boys," Sergeant Henderson said, and I nodded. In truth, though, I'd lost my urge to shoot anybody. I stumbled on through the enemy camp, confused. Were these pitiful wretches the same men who had taken the Alamo, who had chased the Texian army nearly to Louisiana?

That camp was a dreadful thing to behold. The Mexican officers tried to form lines with their frantic men, but our riflemen cut down one bunch after another. A fair portion of the Mexican army never got 10 paces from their tents that day. I saw dead men still dressed in their nightshirts or drawers.

Near the edge of the lake, where Sherman's regiment had driven a hundred or so of the enemy into the water, some of the Mexicans had formed a final line. I found myself staring at two young drummers nervously banging out a steady tempo with their sticks. They continued to summon their army to battle as older men fell on every side of them. Finally the men forming the left of the line threw down their muskets and begged for mercy. When one of our men found a red kerchief tied to one of the Mexican bayonets, he waved it in their faces. Not one of them was spared.

I made my own charge at the drummers. I yelled for them to surrender, but they didn't understand. A Mexican officer moved over to block my path. He was already bleeding from both thighs, but he waved his sword at me. His effort lacked force, though, and I knocked his weapon aside with my rifle. The drummers then raised their hands.

Sergeant Henderson took charge of the officer, and I forced the drummers to toss aside their sticks and discard their drums.

"Hold on there!" Grandpa Nelson shouted, marching toward us. "No quarter, remember?"

"Not them," I insisted, swinging my rifle at the old man.

"Look at them, son!" Grandpa Nelson urged. "They're old as you are! Old as my little grandsons were."

"*Their* side called no quarter, not ours," Andrew reminded me.

"We didn't say it, though," I replied. "We're not like them, are we?" I asked Andrew. "We're not murderers."

"What would your pa say about that?" Grandpa Nelson asked.

"I think he'd say there's been enough dying," I said, shuddering. "Would he be right?" I asked, pointing at the dead scattered across the Mexican camp.

"Maybe," Grandpa Nelson said, sheathing his knife and resting a heavy hand on my shoulder.

Another group of soldiers appeared, eager to have at the drummers, but Colonel Sherman himself took charge of the boys. I rested easier knowing they were safe.

"I always knew you were crazy," Andrew told me afterward. "But that was beyond crazy even for you!"

"I owed a debt," I explained. "Two of them. Two of us. Don't you figure it that way?"

He dropped his chin onto his chest and nodded.

"You're a hard person to figure, Jeff, but I'm getting to

where I trust your instincts. Truth is, I'm tired of the killing too."

We passed the balance of the afternoon guarding prisoners. I wasn't sure if we were preventing escapes or keeping our own companions from killings them, though. By and by the blood-lust passed, and a sense of charity seemed to come over our army. Nearly half the Mexican army, 700 souls, were herded into a makeshift prison pen. Another 600 were dead, and 200 wounded lay in a hospital of sorts, tended by our doctors and their own. Only a handful of the enemy escaped.

One great mystery remained, though. Where was Santa Anna? El Presidente had seemingly vanished. We heard stories that he had ridden off to bring in reinforcements that afternoon. Many of the prisoners insisted that he was dead. Seguin's men—who knew Santa Anna by sight—searched the dead, wounded, and prisoners, but the most hated man in Texas was not among any of them.

If he had done any fighting that day, I hadn't seen it. Our soldiers had looted his tent, locating his uniform and medals. One rumor had him enjoying the company of a slave girl when the battle began. If that was true, that girl should have gotten a medal, because we never would have done so well against an organized defense.

We did do well too. Only two of our men were killed outright. A few others died of their wounds, and others would have scars to show for their day's labor. We had utterly destroyed the enemy, though. And we had evened the score for the hundreds of our own men slain in the battles farther west and in the Goliad massacre. But without Santa Anna, the fighting would go on. We all knew that.

# Chapter 12

## The Road to Reunion

That night and the next morning, our cavalry continued to round up stray Mexicans hiding in the tall grass and along the shore. When one of them appeared in our camp, wearing torn britches but a fine silk shirt, we knew something was going on. Mexican soldiers stood at attention and some muttered, "El Presidente."

Santa Anna tried to square his shoulders and put on a brave face, but he was a beaten man. He must have known there were Texians eager to kill him. He wasn't prepared for the bloodthirsty cries of our little army, though.

So at last, the great villain of my story was finally in the hands of his enemies. There was a general feeling that we should hang the rascal, but General Houston insisted that we spare Santa Anna. There could be no peace without a surrender. In return for his life, the president of

Mexico recognized an independent Texas that stretched from the Sabine and Red rivers to the Rio Grande.

I learned all that later, though. Having never officially joined the Texian army, I handed in my rifle, bid Andrew and the rest of my company farewell, and set off to locate my family. The trip was long and difficult, and I might have given up, but I knew it was an obligation I owed Pa. After escaping General Urrea's cavalry and reaching the Brazos, I deemed myself up to the effort.

I was maybe 30 miles east of San Jacinto when I spied Maddy and Frank fishing along the banks of the Trinity River. It took me a moment to be sure it was them. Maddy seemed older, and little Frank was no longer the shrimp of a nine-year-old I had left two months before. I must have looked frightful because when I called to them, they dropped their poles and ran for cover.

To them, of course, I must have been a ghost, for nobody who had been with Fannin was believed still alive. When I finally located Ma and Mrs. Sagler, they both wrapped their arms around me and hugged me tightly.

"We feared you were dead!" Ma exclaimed as she looked me over. "You smell of sweat and gunpowder. You need a good scrubbing and a haircut."

"Yes, ma'am," I agreed. "It's been a hard trip."

"And your father?" she asked.

I drew out of my pocket the water-stained and wrinkled letter I had carried from Goliad. Much of the ink had run, and it was difficult for her to make out all the words. I suppose she got the gist of it, though.

"He died a soldier?" she finally asked.

"He was murdered," I said, shivering as the rage returned. "They led them out and shot them. After the surrender, Ma."

"And did you find my man?" Mrs. Sagler asked. "And Seth and Sam?"

"Seth died of a wound he received at Coleto Creek," I told her. "Sam and his pa were with my pa. They're all of them dead, ma'am," I said, brushing a tear from my eye. "I wish it wasn't so, but it is."

"I thank you for the news, Jefferson," she said, squeezing my shoulder. When I winced, Ma located my wound and got the rest of the story out of me. When I got to the part about Josh, I could hold back my tears no longer.

"Wasn't your fault," Mrs. Sagler said when I turned back to her. "All my boys are headstrong. I am myself."

I marveled that she could maintain her composure, but Andy and Spence told me later that she cried most of the night.

Ma boiled water and produced a cake of soap for me. I considered myself too old to be bathed by a mother, so she sent Maddy along with the tub into a clump of willows. Frank brought me clean clothes. Except for Alejandro's shoes, which still had some leather in their soles, I discarded my old outfit. My brothers were fascinated by the scar left by the Mexican musket ball, but I really couldn't talk to them about the fighting—either at Coleto Creek or at San Jacinto, as the last battle became known.

Somehow they seemed to understand and didn't ask me about it again for a long time.

That night we sat together around a fire with the Saglers. Moses, Harriet, and Abner had been there too, but Mrs. Sagler sent them west toward Columbia to prepare for our homecoming. It saddened me to realize that so many faces were missing, but Annie came over and sat beside me. She always had a sweet voice, and she sang "Home Sweet Home" as Spence Sagler blew the tune on his mouth organ.

"I've missed you, little sister," I told her afterward. She gave me a hug and a kiss, and I replied in kind.

The trip back to Columbia took us nearly a week. Our neighbors had welcomed General Urrea's cavalry the week before. Now they professed gratitude for our two families' sacrifices. They brought us livestock and food to ease the burden of our losses. Even Wes Hamilton was civil to me.

In May, Ma received a certificate from the new Texas government for 640 acres of land. At General Houston's insistence, I got one too, for my service at San Jacinto. We sold Pa's certificate for cash to buy 200 acres along the Brazos from Mrs. Sagler.

There would be some hard times ahead for us. I think we all knew that. We would be a time mourning Pa and growing accustomed to our new home, but I knew we would come through all right in the end. The Byrds might have itchy feet, but as Ma liked to say, we weren't all Byrd. She was a Hall, and they were accustomed to building futures in far-flung places.

It didn't really dawn on me that we were home until one morning when Maddy and I were chopping stove wood down by the river. By then the last Mexican armies had turned homeward, and most of our prisoners taken at San Jacinto had slipped away and made their way back to Mexico or signed on as hired hands at the settlements along the Brazos and Colorado Rivers. Maddy took to singing as he worked, and I recognized the tune as a fresh one, a ballad about a young soldier and the girl he had left behind.

Ma stepped out to listen, and I could see her wipe her eyes once or twice. When we were finished with our work, Maddy went to look after the cows we had recently bought. I joined Ma on the porch.

"You know," I told her, "I met a girl in Goliad. She saved my life."

"I suspected you might have had some help," she said, "Tell me about her."

I found it difficult to sort the story from my feelings, but I gave her a half-decent account of my time with the Espinosa family and of Carla in particular.

"You know, Jeff," she said, "if we're going to make a life for ourselves here, we'll need more than a few cows and a few acres of corn. I know you've always been troubled a bit by horses, but what would you think of raising saddle mounts?"

"Maddy's good with animals," I told her. "There are plenty of good animals hereabouts to start with too."

"I hear that the Spanish brought real thoroughbreds to Texas, though," she told me. "Arabians. I wonder if we might not buy a good stallion from down around Goliad, say."

"Might be a good idea," I agreed.

"You might take your brother along and have a bit of an adventure, the two of you. I think it would do Maddy good. You too, perhaps. I suspect there's a certain young lady down south who would enjoy learning you made it home."

"After fighting the Mexican army, I don't know that I'd still be welcome."

"Sooner or later we all of us have to do what we can to bring this new country of ours together," she said, kissing my forehead. "Sometimes it's easier to fight a battle than to make a nation."

"We've made our own beginning here, haven't we?" I asked.

"Yes, . . . but horses! That's a real future."

"To be honest, I wouldn't mind making that trip to Goliad, Ma. I hear the road's a little better now."

"So it's said. And Jeff, when you reach the place where your father lies, would you find a rose to place there in his memory."

"Don't you think you should do that yourself?" I asked.

"I've already made my peace with Randolph," she insisted. "Now it's time for you and Maddy to do the same. I know your father's loss has given you extra burdens to carry, but it's made you both strong. I miss my little boys sometimes, but I'm awfully proud of the men they're becoming."

I couldn't help smiling. It was hard to consider that all was right with the world, not with Pa dead and so many others too. I couldn't gaze up the hill and not remember Josh. But Ma was right about making a new beginning, and if I was still a ways from being a man, I was getting there. I did my part, after all, even when it was hard. That's what—Pa had told me often enough—a man did.

There were no comets in the sky those days, but there was a new country to build. It would be hard work, but I wasn't afraid of it. With Ma, Maddy, Frank, and Annie to offer their love and aid, I figured we could manage. It was time to grow taller, work hard, and perhaps find some peace.

# Authors Note

Like most of the soldiers who served the Texas cause at San Jacinto, I am not a native of the state. My own parents brought me to Dallas in the early 1950s in search of the same dream of a better future that drew so many others in 1835 and afterward. The history of my adopted state is a part of my own identity, and I always take delight in writing about it.

Except for the historical figures in this story, most of the characters are representations of the lesser-known individuals who played such important, if less dramatic, roles in the fight for Texas independence. There were, for example, many survivors of the Goliad massacre, and many of them would not have lived if not for the aid offered by the Tejano ranchers of the region. Not all American settlers in Texas supported the revolt, and the citizens of Columbia spared their town by pledging their loyalty to Mexico. Houston's army was often on the verge of rebellion, and there was, without question, much unnecessary killing at San Jacinto. Considering the mood of the Texians, perhaps we should deem it fortunate that half the Mexicans present *were* taken prisoner.

I have relied, where possible, on original accounts as the basis of this story. For the episodes in and around Goliad, I used the diaries of Abel Morgan and Dr. J. H. Barnard, both *medicos* spared the fate of so many. I am also indebted to Newton Warzecha and the staff at the restored

Presidio La Bahia at Goliad for their kindness and hard work in illuminating the events of February and March 1836.

No visitor to the tall spire that marks the battlefield at San Jacinto can help but marvel at the good fortune enjoyed on April 21 by Sam Houston's Texians. After the battle, a Mexican officer observed that perhaps the ghosts of the dead from the Alamo and Goliad had risen to secure that victory. Most students of the battle attribute the Texas success to Santa Anna's bungling. Even so, the battle remains one of the most decisive and one-sided in the history of North America.